LIVEWIRE
from THE WOMEN'S PRESS

Sandra Chick is 24 and lives in the West Country. This is her first novel.

Sandra Chick

Push Me, Pull Me

First published by The Women's Press Limited 1987
A member of the Namara Group
34 Great Sutton Street, London EC1V 0DX

Reprinted 1987 (twice)

British Library Cataloguing in Publication Data
Chick Sandra
Push me, pull me
1. Title
823'.914 [F] PZ7
ISBN 0-7043-4901-9
Typeset by M.C. Typeset Limited, Chatham, Kent
Printed and bound by Hazell Watson & Viney Ltd, Aylesbury, Bucks

I would like to thank everyone at The Women's Press for their support. I am especially grateful to my editor, Robyn Slovo.

I also want to thank Nevil for his encouragement throughout.

One

Everyone likes Christmas Eve. I don't. Would never admit it though, wouldn't be fair on the others to play selfish and dampen the spark. Truth is, I get jealous of the fun everybody else is having. Only like the presents, just pretend to enjoy the rest. Can't stand pushing myself forward I s'pose. You know, stupid games, dancing, that kind of thing. Makes me feel clumsy and embarrassed, makes my cheeks flush and a sort of cramped sensation belts me in the stomach. I wish I didn't feel that way. I'd like to join in, be the one who's always there, in the centre, but I can't force myself. The more people try to encourage me, the bigger idiot I feel. Prefer my own company – quite happy but in a different way.

It was chilly out, still had my jacket on, collar turned up to cover my ears, hands pushed up inside the front – didn't have pockets or gloves. I let my tongue taste the clearness that crept down on to my lip from my nose, cold and itchy – always do that and hope no one ever sees. When it's really freezing my eyes go funny, and they were sort of stiff from the bitter wind. It was one of those alive nights, the walk home was good if nothing else. The grass was crunchy, the sound reminded me of screwing up the see-through paper that comes on chocolate boxes. It glistened, as if it'd been sprayed with artificial frost. I love the clacking of metal-tipped heels and toes against shiny pavements. It was icy, the rain had formed a sheet of glass, the thin tread of my shoes skated against it. Nice to be in the warm though, looking out.

'How's she feeling?' he said.

'Mum? Don't know. I've just come in.'

'Out late.'

'Not really, it's only nine.'

'Oh. Thought it was later.'

He locked the door behind himself.

'Get the fire on then.'

Didn't register until I heard him ping the switch down, not intending to wait for ever. My turn to speak.

'Think it'll snow?'

'Doubt it. Not cold enough for that.'

'Mum said it was *too* cold.'

'Yeah, well. Either way, makes no difference to me.'

Felt like there should have been something more important to talk about than the weather but we never found much to say. Could have made an effort but didn't. He wandered, a bit awkward, before his shadow joined mine at the kitchen window.

'Nothing on telly?'

'Might be, haven't looked.'

'See the state of him out there.'

I'd noticed them on my way home, an Arabian knight, a cowboy and a vicar. They'd been in front and I'd gone slow so's not to catch up. The cowboy had strayed or been left behind and was slumped on the kerbside opposite. He bent double and heaved, a sea of puke spilling from his mouth. The load in his belly spurted out in jets like it'd never stop.

'Bad as her. Had a right skinful earlier on.'

'I know. I hate to see Mum like that.'

He kind of laughed, but not out loud.

'She's all right.'

'I didn't mean that she's not. I meant, I hate to see Mum like that.'

'Well, she's entitled to a good time, especially now.'

'What's good about it? Shouldn't have to get unconscious.'

'That's up to her.'

'Makes a fool of herself.'

'Like I said, her business. She's of age.'

'Yeah, it's no reason though, no excuse is it?'

'What's got into you tonight? Forget it. And anyway, young lady, I wonder what Santa Claus has in store?'

'Dunno. Not much, Mum can't afford much can she?'

'She's better off than a lot. She's got a job.'

'I know but she's got . . . '

'Some of us haven't. Nearly four million haven't.'

I gave in, wasn't worth it.

'No. I s'pose you're right.'

'Bloody fascists . . . '

The cowboy tried to stand.

'Be the do at The Bell.'

'That where you've been?'

'Typical. What makes you think I've been to the pub?'

I shrugged. Didn't care where he'd been. Only conversation. Knew he'd been drinking – as he spoke the beer fumes smelt high, his breath against mine. He moved away, off into the front room. The television went from channel to channel.

'Waste of bloody energy,' he said, not to me, or at least I didn't comment. I stayed there, watching. Mum was right – there were a lot of people about despite the bad roads, though I'd say that more than usual had opted to walk. The yellow street lamps made them all look sick. Or perhaps they all *were* sick, I don't know.

The odd burst of enthusiasm, a cheer of approval. Down in the street a bottle smashed.

'After three. Three. Once in Royal David's City . . . '

The voices of the Arabian knight and the vicar merged together with small-town noises as they came back to collect the lost merrymaker.

'Now the holly bears a berry as red as the . . . '

'No. As white as the . . . '

'What?'

'As white as the . . . '

'Milk.'

'Milk?'

'As white as the spunk, and we wish you a merry Christmas and a ha-ppy new year.'

I slammed the window shut, the fresh air isn't, not around our way. Not smoky or smelly, just dirty with people. Slammed it hard, made things shake. Wanted them to go away for ever. They heard me and looked up. One of them started whistling, the music of 'The Stripper'. I ignored it, glanced up the road, avoiding their stare to act like I'd not noticed and hadn't been concerned with them anyway. Don't think they saw Bob reappear behind me, he was out of the light. If they did he didn't bother them anyway, the vicar called out to me, already hoarse.

'Oh Grandma – what beautiful eyes you have! Oh Grandma – what beautiful hair you have! Oh Grandma – what beautiful big tits you have!'

They fell into each other and giggled, pointing and waving.

'What have we here then? Is it Daddy Christmas? Is it a snowman? No! It's the Virgin Mary!'

There were whispers before they shouted out again, a couple of private jokes.

'Don't think she wants to know us lads, never mind, all together now – Jingle Balls . . . '

Bob was mad.
'Come away. Draw the curtains.'
As I turned around we collided. He didn't smile, but then we rarely smiled. That same old expression – I recognised it straight off, there again to haunt me. For a second or two I was stone, crumbling stone.
'How about a Christmas kiss then?'
I tried to pass it over, even grinned I think.
'No. Not Christmas Day yet.'
He lifted one hand, pressed between thumb and forefinger was about half an inch of cigarette, flattened by the pressure. He offered me a drag. I shook my head, tried to wriggle past him. He was bigger than ever before, I was smaller than ever before. He blew his smoke into my face, did it on purpose.
'Just once more.'
'No, Bob.'
'This'll be the last time, I promise.'
His hands cupped my jaw.
'I won't do it properly. We'll do the same as before. Come on, won't hurt you. What you afraid of?'
I shrank tight all over.
'I don't want to. I hate it. And Mum.'
'Why? Didn't harm you. What *would* your mother say – what d'you think?'
'Stop it.'
'Shhh, baby, it's all right. Look, it's only touching. That can't be wrong can it?'
I could feel the sweat tickle my armpits and crawl in the hollow of my back. Boom, boom, boom, in my heart, in my head. He kissed me. The taste was stale and rancid, sent my stomach growling, round and round, round and round. A film of slobber plastered my face.
'Please. Don't make me.'
'Shhh . . . '
Inside felt strained and twisted.

'Not properly. You said . . . '

'No. Come on, I won't, the same as before.'

Oh please God.

He acted as if he was starved. It was pathetic, the way I was squeaking like a toy doll, then gasping with no sound.

'No. *Please don't.*'

I let myself go loose to make the hurt less. It made it easier for him, let him do as he wanted. Get it over quickly. Christ, I didn't know it was going to be like this.

He spoke.

'Here, stop that sniffin'.'

Gave me his hanky. I wiped my eyes, my nose, my dribbling mouth. Wanted to cancel him away.

'Bob, *you did it,* the whole thing. Said you *never* would.'

'Shhh, that's the last time, promise. Promise not to tell?'

We both knew there was no chance of that.

'Good girl.'

I lay there, curled, crumpled in a heap. He reached out, pulled me to sit. Kneeling forwards against the swaying floor, a mass of glue oozed on to my bare legs.

'Where's Mum?'

'Shhh, you're a big girl now.'

I didn't want to be a big girl. I wanted my mum. Felt queasy and ill, couldn't stand. Couldn't stop the gushing warm pee, the shame or the stink.

Bob had gone. But he was still there, everywhere, I saw him, felt him, heard his panting. I ached and shivered. Oh please God, let there be a pain, let there be cancer, but don't let there be a tomorrow. All I could think about was Mum, whimpering for her, needing her, but not wanting her to come, see.

As it turned out she was still drunk from the

lunchtime, completely crashed out on the sofa. She'd been there all the time. I pulled my clothes on as best I could, went upstairs, washed myself. Bathed slowly, like always, except usually it was only my hands that smelt dirty and tangy. I hid my jeans, they were stained and wet. Brushed the knots out of my hair, went to bed. I covered my head with the pillow, the quietness was too loud. I cried. Cried until the colourless dawn came.

I love my mum. She's not a bad woman – I know some people think that she is, people that don't really know her. Auburn perm and shiny beige skin, a bit lumpy in places. When I look at her it's difficult to believe that she's given me my life, that once I was inside of her body. Quite often we don't get on too well but only because we're honest with each other and there's nothing wrong with that. She used to be decidedly fat, then was just slender I s'pose. Now, I think she's craggy and bony – her neck is all creased and her cheeks sag.

'Thin is beautiful.' *She* says. Likes herself better that way but I don't. I think she doesn't want to get old but makes herself look even older than she really is.

Mum always slices bread on a slant impossible to follow and she winges on about things that are none of her concern. Everyday irrelevancies are carefully filed somewhere in her head, she's the ability to locate and recall the mistakes of others with complete one-sidedness to suit her mood. Happens often, with the exaggeration of more unpleasant issues. I hate the way that she peels the silver foil from hot food, how she coughs unnecessarily and how she makes out never to hear a question on first asking. Yet the light follows her around, she glows. I don't think I'd ever get by without her. Home is where we both belong. A place where fuss is never far away – it has to be like that so's to keep everything moving steadily along, as it always has done. Change is unwelcome. Sometimes I call Mum by her christian name, Stephanie, Steph for short. Bob prefers to concentrate on the latter part referring to her as Fanny, or occasionally, Stuff-me or Stuffanny. Thinks it's amusing.

She's always worked. Always worked damn hard too. When she couldn't get a job that paid enough, she trained for one. When one job wasn't enough, she got two. Been a machinist in a factory that makes overalls, a shop assistant, primary school cleaner, a general clerk at a transport company. Nothing brilliant but you have to get money from somewhere to keep a house going. Bob's limited, can't do most jobs, a problem with his back. Gets Mum to rub it for him when it's really bad, but it can't hurt too much, they always end up larking about, tickling each other then kissing, he'll stick his hand down the front of her jumper. I can't stand to see them doing stuff like that. Once I screamed at them to stop it but they only laughed and teased, said I was 'green'. In the end Bob got angry, called me 'spoiled' and 'too sensitive for my own good'. It's just that when I see Mum doing things like that she's different. It's like she's, I don't know, a man-eater or something.

When people ask me what she's like, I tell them 'dead clean'. Got very little to call her own, but what she's got she's earnt, and she's proud of it. Spends every penny that comes along, more often than not on really crass things – stuff that's meant to look old fashioned but is obviously brand new. And we always seem to have loads of cushion covers, and chair covers, the stretchy ones. Her favourite colours are orange and black. The household itself is, well, modest, but okay, or at least it would be okay if less of the things made me cringe – ornaments, 'A gift from sunny Torquay', 'Greetings from Barry Island'. I tell her that the place looks good because it's all she's got really and it's what she wants to hear. Poured her entire life into her home, wherever that home happens to have been. And as I said, she's worked damn hard. Lets herself go at times too, feels she qualifies for that luxury at least. Normally everything is spotless, not necessarily tidy but never mucky, well not often, 'cept her room. One of her most frequent sayings is 'haven't got the time'. There never seems to be enough time does there? If it's not the rituals of domestic duty on her mind, I'll bet anything it's me. Well, mostly.

Even so, it's not the same as it used to be. It's like everything's been tipped upside down and shaken about. I feel as if I know everything and yet nothing at the same time. Don't claim to know what I want for myself but I know what I don't want. And what I think about things, serious things, and exactly why I believe what I do. Not many people seem to be able to back their arguments – that's not right. It's no good to spout about something if inside you've got no reasons. I read all I can, watch the six o'clock news and programmes like that – even if they sound boring, sometimes you get a surprise. Mum and Bob say that I read crap and watch crap. Mum usually switches over if the going gets too heavy, especially if there's a comedy on. Says she needs a good laugh to relax, forget the day's work, forget tomorrow's work, all her problems. I never see her laughing though, she just complains about the 'bloody rubbish on telly today' and by how much the licence fee is rumoured to be increasing in the next year. Government, politics, Mum says shouldn't matter to ordinary people like us, we can't do anything to change the situation so there's no point in finding out or getting involved. Bob's told me a hundred times that I should stop pretending to be brainy when I'm as thick as Mum really.

That's when I start thinking that I know nothing,

when someone says something like that. Think that I'm too dumb to see that what they're saying is true. But I believe in change. Trouble is, before something new can come, something old has to go. And it's not that simple, if you can't get to the people with influence you might as well forget it. I know it's easier not to bother. Mum's rude to politicians when they're on telly, calls them names, hurls any abuse she can think of, but I bet if she met one in the street she'd be 'Yes sir, no sir'.

So when Bob implies that I'm an idiot, I shut up. Have no way of standing up and proving to him that I'm not stupid – perhaps I am. I don't think Mum is, not really. That's why I never bite, it'd be saying, 'Yes, I'm thick like Mum', or, 'No, I'm not thick, even if Mum is'. I'm not sure if I don't have the answers because I'm not intelligent enough to figure them out, or if it's because I'm bright enough to see that what some people call answers are actually excuses and ways of blaming mistakes on to someone else. Blame is useless. It's for big mouths who don't know how to repair things.

In one way I want to learn more – I wish I knew somebody who thinks like me, feels like me, yet when anyone does try to help I leap to my own defence and reject them. Hate being told. I'd rather do the telling. Reckon I can be spiteful. A fool. Bob says I should keep my mind on the *real* world, respect the attitudes of those folk with experience, i.e. him. I think it works both ways, that a younger person can teach someone older too. I can hurt in the same way as them, but they don't understand that. I know about some things. What it's like to be lonely, feel ugly. They'd probably say I was wrong, don't know the meaning of the words and to shut my gob. But if they do understand those things, why didn't this great mysterious wisdom see what was happening, why didn't they prepare me for them? I s'pose that different people have different priorities, they've got bills and that to worry about, but it's all to do with survival.

When I leave school Mum wants me to get a 'job for life', meaning one where I'm unlikely to be made redundant. The food line would be secure then, she's decided. Everyone would eat. Except if they live in Africa. Bob says I might as well've finished my schooling long ago, exams are a waste of time and energy when there's no work to be had at the end. Mum never mentions exams, always assumes that I'm not going to pass any subjects so there's no point. But I don't want to be a convenience, I want to stand up and be me, I want to be *someone*. I want to be famous.

When I come close to achieving something worthwhile, something almost half good, I try to kick others down, I like them to fall so as to make my accomplishment all the more remarkable. I know that Mum's disappointed with me, says I talk like a snob. That confuses me. I wouldn't mind so much if she didn't like me, love me, but she does and to disappoint her is the worst thing I could possibly do to insult her. Trouble is, it's all too late now, we don't come together the same, we don't share. I don't even trust her with things that really matter. Hasn't been the same since Bob moved in with her, us. He took over, at last he'd 'got her', 'got his woman'. He's caught her, has her surrounded, but that doesn't mean he'll get what he wants. It means he'll destroy some bits of her. And maybe lose all the things he liked. Nothing becomes clearer, I've just got used to the fog.

Our kitchen's always been a stage, entertainment for the neighbourhood.

'I've burnt the bloody turkey. For Christ's sake don't just sit there, Bob. Help me. Or go and get that lazy sod out of bed – it's gone two o'clock.' Mum should have been a town crier.

Today was a day like any other. Except it was Christmas. Except when I woke up this morning I'd messed my knickers. When I washed, it clogged under my nails and made me want to throw up.

'Oi, move yourself . . . '

It was *him*, Bob, bawling up the stairs.

'I have done. I'm washing.'

It itched between my legs, I didn't want to touch myself so I soaped the sponge and used that instead.

'Spending the bloody day in there?'

'I'm coming.'

Mum chipped in, ' 'Bout time. Self, self, self – think of others for a change.'

I didn't know how to face them, couldn't look at either. I was so frightened, so ashamed. I'd still expected one glance then Mum would go sickly pale, 'Oh no, what the hell's happened? Oh my God, Bob . . . ' She'd start crying and hold me tight against her, tell me that everything was going to be all right.

The kitchen was stifling, hazy with steam. I couldn't speak.

'Stir that gravy, Catherine, got lumps in it now . . . '

'Where's my fags?'

'Never mind your fags, Bob, get some knives and forks out. What's the bloody time?'

'Where's my fags? Where's the puddin'? Take ages, better get it boiling or it'll never be ready.'

She sighed. 'Get the knives and forks, PLEASE.'

'I see. You didn't get one did you? I don't believe it, the last thing I said to you as you walked out the door . . . '

'Bob . . . '

'Well, I told you – *make sure you get a puddin'*. Didn't I?'

'Didn't have time, didn't know you like 'em all that much, now get those things on the table, PLEASE.'

'You're bloody hopeless. Don't listen to a word I say, might as well not bother.'

'*Bob* . . .'

'Where's my fags? You had 'em?'

'Put the telly on, the Queen'll be on soon.'

'Do this Bob, do that Bob, unpaid servant that's what I am, bloody slave. Ought to start charging.'

'So when do you get *your* money this week?'

'Dunno.'

'Bob, you said you'd find out, we've got the . . .'

'Yes. All right. I'll go down there. What d'you want me to do – stand outside until they all come back from the holiday?'

'I'm only . . . '

'I know, you're only saying.'

Dinner was on the table. It was three o'clock. The Queen was on the telly. I prayed there was still time to wake up and find myself dead. No such luck.

The front room smelt cabbagey.

'Might get a car.'

'Who might?'

'I might.'

'What d'you mean, Bob, you might get a car?'

'It's perfectly bloody simple woman – I said I might get a car; you know, four wheels, brum brum.'

'Have you any idea how much it'll cost to run a car?'

'Seen one in the paper, only a hundred and fifty.'

'And tax, and insurance.'

'Meat's dry.'

'Repairs, MOT.'

'Sprouts're bloody hard.'

'Petrol . . .'

The tip-tap of stainless steel against plates. A posh lady's speech from a brown plastic box in one corner. No one heard, no one cared. Eat, eat, eat. Sit, wait, expect, demand. Never owe, never give anything, only take, grab. Mum was annoyed and a bit upset, turned her dinner over with the fork but didn't get through much. I picked as usual. Bob pigged himself.

'So, there's no pudding then?'

'There's some fruit if you . . . '

'Don't care for bloody fruit, tinned crap.'

'Coffee?'

'No. Tea.'

Mum put the kettle on, left Bob and me at the table. I couldn't even lift my head up, felt humiliated, guilty.

'The trouble with your mother is, she won't put herself out.'

'She works hard, Bob.'

'Yeah. My ass.'

I closed my eyes, remembered how, once, I thought it'd be. Tender, that's what I thought. Not empty, not a million years of empty. The tea arrived, too soon, too late or just in time.

'Sugar, Bob?'

'Course I want sugar, always have sugar.'

'You said you were cutting down that's all.'

'For God's sake, it's Christmas, course I want sugar.'

He unloaded three heaped teaspoonfuls into his Capricorn mug, black and gold, too nice for him, didn't suit his grip, those hands, strangling thick fingers.

'Any decent films on the box?'

'Dunno.'

'Have a look, then.'

'You look, you wanna know.'

Mum passed the paper to him, opened at the right page.

'Why the hell d'you have to turn everything inside out?'

She didn't answer, went through to the kitchen, didn't like the gutsing any more. I saw a tear in her eye but her face was hard. Seemed ages before she came back, don't think it was that long. Her lashes were clogged with blue.

'Right, love, let's open the pressies shall we?'

The two of us knelt together in front of the fire. I'd given Mum some perfume. She was pleased, spraying herself around the neck and on each wrist. Bob pretended to be distraught with the fumes. I gave him twenty fags, secretly hoping they'd speed up his departure. Mum had bought me some make-up (my first), a jumper and some underwear. For a while she acted like a girl again, all excitable.

'Try the sweater, love.'

'Here?'

'Course, silly.'

I stooped behind the sofa, pulled my shirt off, the jumper on.

'Oh, Bob, look at that, doesn't she look smashin' ? Oh, you look fabulous. Do like it, don't you? '

'Yeah, it's great. Thanks, Mum.'

We sort of kissed though our lips never touched.

'Thank Bob too, love.'

'Thanks, Bob.'

'Good. She likes it, Bob. Keep it on, love.'

Bob was watching a poxy circus.

'What've you got for Mum, Bob?'

He stayed quiet, Mum whispered, 'Love, you know Bob hasn't been able to get work for, for I don't know how long. And what's that mark, love?'

I was ready.

'Fell over last night.'

'How?'

'Slipped on the ice.'

'Had a tipple round at that Sophie's more like. Hear that, Bob? Little sod. Had a drink last night, fell over. Don't get in that state too often. Still it's your Christmas as well, every right to enjoy yourself, eh?'

She smiled. Bob was asleep. His shirt was open at the chest and bottom. That clammy skin watched me, dared me, threatened me.

'Next door have gone to church. Fancy going to church *today*. You do like the pullover don't you? Yeah, you do, I can tell.'

I wanted to thump Mum. Hated her for not just knowing, I shouldn't have to tell her.

It stung each time I had a wee. There was a spot of blood on my pants but not much.

Gran was coming round early evening. She'd bring something for me, something nice, I was sure. Till then I had more to think about than usual, less to say. Made out I had a cold. As it turned out, she was before time – arrived at five instead of six like she'd said. 'Can't stop long', like always.

'For your school work,' said the overcoat that pongs of TCP.

I unwrapped it quick and was a bit disheartened, though tried to sound enthusiastic.

'A dictionary! Thanks, Gran.'

Gave her a hug. Wasn't allowed to go upstairs – rude, Mum said, so I made sure to get an end seat on the sofa so's no one could see what words I was looking up. Mastiff, mastitis, mastodon, mastoid, *masturbate*, produce sexual orgasm or arousal by manual stimulation of genitals, etc. I wish they wouldn't say 'etc.' as if everyone knew what they meant by it. Vagabond, vagal, vagary, *vagina*, canal between womb and external genital orifice of female. Canada, canaille, canakin, *canal*, artificial watercourse for inland navigation or irrigation. *Canal boat*, long narrow boat for use on canals.

The front room looked nice, the tree in one corner, real good. Gran noticed too. We'd bought some fresh tinsel (needed it) but didn't let on to Bob, he hadn't wanted us to trim up – waste of money. It's not the only secret Mum kept from him. She told me that he wanted her to have a baby and she'd gone on taking her pills without him knowing. Blamed her age for infertility if he questioned her. If that was me I'd've said – quite simply – that I didn't *want* a baby. Things seem to get so complicated when you're older. I hate to think of *him* doing *that* to my mum. I wonder how many men she's done it with? Five? Ten? Twenty? More? I've no idea what the normal amount is. Once I found a black stocking in her bed and cried because I thought it meant she was some kind of whore – course I was *much* younger then. She told me that she wasn't, said that before tights were invented everybody wore them. But she did say that I mustn't go in her room looking around again. I only hope she doesn't enjoy it, that'd be horrible. She never talks to me about sex really, not the details, not about how you do it, what it's meant to feel like.

It was nothing like I'd expected, it was the most terrible thing I can imagine. Perhaps she doesn't tell me because Bob says so often how incredibly immature I am for my age. Maybe she thinks I'm too young, wouldn't catch on or might rush out and try it. But thirteen–fourteen – it's quite old really. I look old anyway. I didn't tell Mum before, in case she cried and called me a liar. How could I tell her? What right did I have to mess things up? I felt sick and shaky, wanted to be on my own but wanted to be held tight too.

I thought Gran was never going home, stood on the doorstep for at least an hour.

'So. No news about the coming year then?'

'News?'

'Announcement.'

'Look, Mum. We've had this out before. I'm buggered if I'll go through it again for you or anybody else.'

'It's the only way.'

'It's a waste of bloody time.'

'No. He'll live off you, sleep in your bed, but will he marry you? Not likely, you're not good enough for that.'

'It's not like that, Mum, and you bloody well know it.'

'Don't know what your father'd say if he were alive.'

'Well he's not, is he.'

It went quiet, always does at the mention of Grandad. Mum was close to him. And Gran was. And me. I piped up.

'I wouldn't want you to marry Bob, Mum.'

'What d'you mean, love, you wouldn't want me to marry Bob?'

'Wouldn't.'

'Why not? What, may I ask, is wrong with Bob?'

'He's a pig.'

'You what! You listen to me, if I catch you saying things like that again, I'll clip your bloody ears.'

'But, Mum, you said you don't *want* to marry Bob.'

'Mind your own business, thank you very much.'

Gran wasn't going to miss this one.

'Needs a father that girl, obvious, and such a shame.'

Mum and Gran were on the same side again, I was in the wrong. I thought I'd been supporting Mum in a battle she was losing. That's what I don't understand – you just can't win. I sloped off to bed in tears but didn't let anyone see, wouldn't give them the pleasure.

Boxing Day we had visitors. Only the two, but right from first thing. Turned into an all-day all-night party, bodies strewn around like grubby washing.

'I'm dreaming of a white . . . '

'Bit bloody late for that . . . '

Bob's step-brother, Stu, grabbed hold of Mum's bum.

'Ooh! Did you see that Bob? Filthy swine.'

'Another drink?'

'How many's that? Ten? Eleven? Worse than your bloody brother you, and he's a handful I can tell you.'

'I'll bet you can.'

'Didn't mean that. 'Nother drinkies, Bob, need I ask?'

She did mean that though, she always says things that really mean *that*. Stu was round with his girlfriend, Julie. Mum's never liked Julie but pretends to so that she can borrow her clothes to wear out. Julie's got tons more clothes than Mum, but then she's single and only seventeen. The four of them started dancing, pushing each other, messing about. Party cans of beer, party LP, party hats. Party, party, party. It was a bomb, a murderer, it was being put in a cage with some wild creature, it was being sent to prison for ever and ever, to rot. Stu disappeared. Came back wearing a pair of Mum's knickers over his trousers. They were in fits. It wasn't funny.

'Bloody hell, Stu!'

'Rather you than me, mate.'

'Always knew there was summat odd about you, Stu.'

'Put 'em on, proper, half measures are no fun.'

'Go on, Stu, I'll stick a fiver on it.'

'On what?'

'Go on, Stu, for a laugh.'

Julie got him around the ankles, pulled his cords down. He had nothing on underneath. They roared clapping and cheering. It was the first time I'd really *seen* a *thing*, I'd always shut my eyes tight.

'You mean you don't wear Y's, Stu!'

'Be prepared, that's what I say.'

'Randy git.'

'Come on, Stu, put the frillies on – get the camera, Steph.'

Tears rolled down their faces as he obliged. Mum snapped away while he jigged about to the music, they were in hysterics. I bet they would have laughed even more to know that I was sat there praying to any god that existed, choking on my own breath.

'They'll never print these . . . '

Stu still had his shoes and socks on, looked so damned ridiculous. I went upstairs, loathing them. And myself. Kept asking the gods to let it be me instead of some hungry, innocent baby in Africa. Mum never meant me any harm but I knew how she'd blab about it all, think it so clever. I felt such a burden to her. The party didn't end till four or five. I was so angry, mad at Mum, why couldn't she see my hurt?

'Always in the bloody bathroom you. Was a time when I couldn't force you, no matter what – afraid of the water then.'

I didn't even mean to be washing, just found myself doing it. Wanted to step out of my skin into new, fresh, clean skin. Inside I screamed – can't you hear me crying out for you? Can't you feel there's something wrong? But if she did come to know, what then? How could I have done it to *her* – stolen her man? She'd be jealous, bitter. The whole world would hear, slack mouths would talk. And draw conclusions. And look at me as I walked in the street, as I worked, as I played. They'd call me names and it'd be true, I'd deserve it.

The day after the party I heard Mum whisper to Julie, 'Upset? No. 'Spect she's got her period.'

Anybody else's Mum would have seen, they'd just look and know. Mine's different – not worse, I don't mean that, but she's had a hard time, a real hard time. Maybe I'm lucky that she has.

The twenty-seventh is a traditional pub day, with 'that lot'. Mum and Bob were out. They invited me along too but I didn't want to go out. Not ever again. In case people could tell. I couldn't bare it – they might not say but I'd know that they knew. I stayed in my room, locked the door, shut them all out. I'm glad to have my own room, I know lots of kids who have to share. I used to stick pictures over the walls but after Mum decorated it wasn't allowed. A bit childish anyway. I never liked the actual room much – sugar and spice and all things nice. Too pink and rosy. Mum got Gran to hitch up the edge of my bedspread and the bottom of my curtains, all fancy, but odd because they were different patterns. I've got brilliant shelves though. Mum couldn't afford the ones I wanted in the shop, so she got a book, borrowed some tools and taught herself how to make them. How to make them well.

According to Mum, mine's always the best room in the house – shows it off to visitors. Clothes all over the floor, never neat. I've got loads to wear, always have had, Mum goes without so's she can give to me. Most of my stuff is from the market stall Bob used to help out on. I don't like to wear a lot of it since some kid at school said he had been sacked for pinching the gear he was supposed to be selling. Mum reckoned they made it all up but I always knew that Bob was a right bastard. I know what bastard means 'cause I looked it up – 1. Born out of wedlock. 2. Resembling another species. 3. A person esp. a man – 'lucky bastard'. He's a real bastard (1.) and a right bastard. And, I swear he resembles an animal. How I'd love to watch him roast at the spit, see the fat run away, burn. Then slice him into pieces, just like he cut me into pieces.

I don't want to be like my mum. I say that, though I'm still scared that I'll become like her without realising until it's too late. She says I shouldn't knock her – that she's doing the best that she can. That this is what life is about, and that I've got a lot to learn. She won't admit it but she thinks she's missed the boat. I don't, and I want her to have the best there is. Think of herself and be proud. I want to be a proud woman. Women should be proud of themselves. I hate to see Mum treated like a piece of muck. She acts like muck sometimes but only because she doesn't rate herself – thinks she's got no real value because that's what men like Bob have told her. When she dresses up to go out she'll always say, 'Do I look all right? Are you sure? D'you think Bob'll like it?'

I wouldn't give a shit whether Bob liked it or not, it's not him whose wearing it. I wish she'd dress for herself and not other people, men. She does herself up so cheap sometimes to try and look sexy but she only manages to look old, I wish she wouldn't do it. Once when we were out somewhere I saw a girl from school. Next day she asked me if that 'tarty' woman I'd been with was my mum. I said I didn't know who she meant – that way I hadn't actually let my Mum down by acknowledging she was common and tarty, but I hadn't admitted to my friend that she was my mother either. I try and walk in front now. She's got an attractive face in her own way, I like it, I know it's wrinkly but so what. She's hung up about her looks since Dad left her for someone else. I read his departing note. One bit said, 'She's everything you're not. Young, smart, pretty . . . '

Mum broke her heart, sobbed. I knew it was that part that'd done it. I put my arms around her, we cried together. But when he'd showed girls off in front of other people, people the two of them had known for years; she went out there and took it – as if she invented control.

I'm sad for Mum, but angry too. Is it love or stupidity? Is she, am I, strong or weak? I try not to criticize what I don't understand, but it seems so pointless, all of it. Just 'being'. I think of the two of them naked, it makes me feel like spewing. There's no reason, I've looked for reasons but can't find the remotest conclusion to offer comfort.

I don't want to be exactly like Mum but I do wish that I knew what fires her, gives her the guts, the will that she's got. And I wish I had some too. I s'pose it's spirit, aimed at the wrong target. I wonder if she cries, cries without sound? I wonder if it's his fault for creating the need, or her fault, my fault for feeding his craving? Feed him, feed him, your life, your blood, your body.

Mum married Bob in the New Year. She was pregnant with his child.

Two

Once I managed to lose myself on a beach crammed with a swarm of dark heads, all detail swallowed up. Sandwiched by blue-green sea and the crowd of faces, I was saved only by the mild touch and gentleness of a lady with mauvish hair and a flabby midriff.

'You lost, love? What does your mummy look like then? Don't cry – oh, come here. What's your name, lovey? Come on, it's all right.'

Her fatness warmed my wet skin and I felt secure again. Lacquered curls brushed stiff against my face, the breeze of late summer hadn't disturbed them one bit. The perfume of her body steals towards me even now. Such broad lips, like they moved of their own accord, a blob of pinkness. Emerald creme had been carefully smoothed over creased lids. Soft hands, with pink nails too, though the coating had started to peel. Spiky hairs poked out from under her arms, greyed by a ring of talcum powder.

'Hey, I know what. Let's buy you an ice cream. D'you like ice cream? Bet you do.'

I didn't want one. Had already gorged two 99s that day. She bought one all the same. The sticks of chocolate they sell you from a van are better tasting than the shop ones.

'Here, look at this.'

She held out the fine silvery chain that hung around her neck. On the end was a small disc, tinny and sharp before you'd even held it.

'See?'

Spinning it she told me that it spelt out the words 'I love you', but you could only read them when the disc span. When it was still, there were just little lines on both sides that made no sense. Then she whispered, 'D'you wanna know something? A secret?'

I nodded. I liked secrets, secrets and fibs.

'Promise you won't tell? Well, I pretend to everyone that someone special gave it to me. You know, someone really very special, like a boyfriend or . . . ' She shrugged and sort of smiled. 'Well. It doesn't matter, it's silly really. I bought it for myself.'

She was far away. I was disappointed, couldn't see what difference it made and started to cry again.

Soon I was back with Mum and Dad. I felt scared clinging to Mum's bare legs, it was my fault that she had cried, I shouldn't have got lost. Her hug was so tight that day, my nose pressed into her, my face squashed up. I can remember the snuffling and closeness, waiting for the shouting, for the smacked bum to smart. I was in a hurry to get it over with but no one acted cross with me and that made it worse. Even then I knew that if I wasn't going to be accused – someone else would be. The initial relief passed. The bickering started as we climbed into the car to leave. Dad in the driving seat.

'You should've been watching her – what the hell were you doing?'

'Here we go, what about you?'

'Always wandering around with your bloody head in the clouds.'

'You're her father, she's your responsibility too.'

'That's it. Blame me. I only work seven days a week. First break I get in months – am I allowed any peace? Oh no. But then, that word's not a familiar one as far as you're concerned is it? Oh, I nearly forgot, can't expect too much.'

'Work? Work? What d'you think I do eighteen hours a day? You're just about the bloody limit.'

'I know what you do all right – anyway – don't blame me for your mistakes.'

'*My* mistakes? *My* mistakes?'

And so it went on, all the way home. I wanted to be separate from them, watched out of the window and at the coloured line up front, the one that showed our speed, one of those that changes – green for slow, orange for middle, red for fast.

Mum licked her hanky and wiped away the impression left on my face from the lady's lipsticky goodbye kiss. When I had referred to her as 'that nice lady' Mum soon corrected me, saying, 'That woman was no lady.'

But she was. So's Mum in her own way. She's kind and radiant; that's what being a real lady means.

That same night, in bed, I felt a weird sensation run all through my body as I thought about the day. As if I'd come dangerously close to something, something terrible and frightening, but I wasn't quite sure what. I recognised that feeling again, at the wedding. It was that same 'lost' feeling. Mum belonged to Bob now. Where did that leave me?

The bride's bedroom was chaotic. It was such an important day for Mum – I never thought she'd recover from the 'hen night' spree with the 'girls' from work. They'd been to a club, Mum'd come back legless, wearing a stupid hat with streamers hanging and had a cold sausage stuffed down her skirt, all greasy and floppy. What a panic it was in the morning. Had her hair done – properly, mind – all curls – cost her ten fifty. Eleven including tip. She usually wears her hair long, lets it dry naturally to go frizzy but that day it was piled up on top, little wringlets here and there. She bought satin knickers and a new bra – one with pads. The dress was cream and frothy, the most wonderful dress I'd ever seen. Ribbons and lace, all apricots and dream topping.

'Mum. You look lovely. Just like . . . a pavlova.'

'I do love Bob, you know. It's going to work out this time.'

The way she said it, it was wrong, as if she was just needing someone to agree with her decision, rather than reassuring me. I smiled at her, with her, for her. She clutched her 'something old' locket in her palm, held it firm against her chest. The sort of locket that people'd fight over when she died.

'Things are gunna be real good for us from now on. Bob's changed. He's more responsible now, he's happy. He'll find a job soon – one that doesn't affect his health, one with no lifting or carting around. P'raps even – after the baby's born – we'll have a holiday. You'd like that.'

'Yeah.'

'Make 'em all jealous at school, that would.'

'Yeah.'

'It'll be nice for you anyway – to have a proper family, like the other kids.'

'Not all of them have.'

'Well, that makes you especially lucky.'

I kissed Mum on the cheek, she was trying.

'Mind me make-up, love.'

'I don't have to call Bob Dad, do I?'

'No, love, not if you don't want to.'

'Oh, I just wondered . . . '

Took ages to fix her up but it was worth it. Felt like the end of something and I was glad we were so private, just me and Mum, nobody else to intrude not even Gran. Us, together, sharing the last moments of times we both treasured. Not sure if she felt it. Though every night when she looks in on me and I pretend to be asleep under the covers, there's a rush of electric between us and I know she's smiling too. Perhaps she's never valued it, though – not in the same way.

I was a sort-of-bridesmaid, you don't have proper ones at a register office. A candy-striped dress resembling a stick of rock, off-white shoes, off-white tights and a (small) bouquet of pale, silk rosebuds. Mum was pretty chuffed with herself that day, I can tell you. I've never seen her look like that before, or since. She was nervous, too, though I can't imagine why – not as if she didn't know him. Her lip wouldn't stop twitching all the way through the service or ceremony, whatever it's called.

The knot in Bob's tie was even bigger than his mouth. I couldn't take my eyes off him. *He* had even made an effort. Nice shirt, new boots, brown suit – three-piece. I wished his lapels would flap, carry him into the air, fly him away at the last second before any commitments could be made. Every bit of hope I had went out to Mum, it was all so perfect, yet none of it quite right. Reckon she thought that being married to him, having his baby would solve everything, but really it meant less money and more expense and a lack of cash would be their biggest problem. Or at least one of them. He'd not alter. You can't make someone be a different person, not for ever, you can't. They can't, and why should they? Gran says that when you're in love you wear blinkers. I can believe that. Mum's just a 'married' sort of woman, not happy or comfortable without a man to cling to, not complete – that's what she thinks anyway. If it hadn't been him I bet it would've been someone else.

The formalities were soon over, didn't seem possible that something so serious could be finalised in such little time. A few snap shots, then everybody piled into different cars, hungry and thirsty.

The reception was at our house. Borrowed some

chairs and tables, pushed them up together in the front room, put white papery cloths on. Hired matching crockery and a load of cutlery from the community centre. Had lovely dried flower arrangements. Cards everywhere. Moved the regular furniture out – suite, telly and all that – stacked it at one end of the kitchen so no trouble when people walked through. Everyone said what a good idea it was.

About thirty were invited, a few relations but mostly friends. Martin and Carol from the pub, Judy and Clive – she calls herself 'a high-class person of leisure' (only jokingly), though Bob calls him 'a bloody moron' for putting up with her. Peter and Wendy – he's the local darts champion, their mantelpiece is overflowing with trophies, their boast is 'more silver than most criminals haul in a lifetime'. That's crap, most of them are wooden. Alan and Suzy – they'd just come back from Tenerife. Mary and Steve – once she wore sandals with five-inch heels – in the snow! Plus she's had a nose job but won't own up. Mum says she's a 'look at me and love me' silly cow. Terry and Hilary – apparently she spreads salad cream on her face to try and improve it, brags that she used to be a model. It's been generally decided that it must have been for shoes. Brian and Liz – he's ten years younger than her! Keith and Sheila – he's in business, can get you anything you want and all at a fraction of the usual price, you just place your order and it comes when it comes.

We got our fridge from him. Oh, and there was Mum's ex, Tony. S'funny, I wondered what they thought when they looked at each other, whether it was about the nights he used to stay, or maybe they weren't important enough to remember. What are you supposed to feel about an ex-person? Embarrassed I should think. I heard them once, ages ago, hadn't really understood why he'd insisted on sharing Mum's room when there was a spare one next to mine, or, for that matter, why he was staying at all when he only lived down the road. I listened out on purpose.

'Careful. Ooh wait. Stop, Tone. I said stop a minute, Tony.'

Silence.

'No. Not like that. Tone, my arm's stuck. Hurry up, I'm tired, got to get up early in the morning.'

Bob hates Tony, calls him a wimp, but he's 'one of the gang' and couldn't be left out.

I was squashed between the wall and Gran's friend Ada. She's pointed with tiny eyes and an abrasive voice box. Reminds me of an alsatian with a sore throat, would be greatly improved if launched into space on the next available shuttle. Deaf as can be, goes on and on because she can't hear the answers to any of the questions she's asking.

'Always nice to have a man about the place isn't it? Not the same without one. Gran's been telling me how well you all get on, that's the main thing, am I right? I do love a wedding don't you, dear? You'd think your mother'd won the pools today wouldn't you? Beautiful. But I do hope she's not going to put too many pickles out, play havoc with me . . . '

Actually, Mum made a good job of the food. Sandwiches – white or brown – cheese, canned salmon, corned beef. Sliced ham, chicken legs. Salad, sausage rolls, egg and bacon flans. Fruit, Black Forest gateau. Sounds a lot but it's surprising how soon it goes.

After the eating came the traditional speeches, pretty well soaked in gin and champagne (so-called), a 'smashing drop of vino' Mum said.

'Ladies and gents, your attention please . . . '

Don't know why but Bob went first, straight into his tale of the rabbi and the air hostess. I felt sick and went outside.

Sometimes I feel like I'll burst if I don't talk to someone. Older people, like those at the wedding, make me feel all childish and bad-mannered. It's like they're my opponents in a huge competition – everyone wants to be liked by everyone else, to please them. Thing is, I don't stand a chance alongside them. They're witty, say real funny things, not rehearsed, they just *are* funny, naturally. They talk about interesting places they've been, or what good times they used to have. Good times never seem to be now times. I haven't been anywhere, done anything, seen anything. I'm so dull in comparison. I wonder if it'll always be the same, if I'll always be dense and if people will avoid being in my company.

Thing is, if I fail, Mum'll think it's because she's failed. But she gets cross when I say I want to change myself. Sometimes she says I should stop being so stubborn and stop dreaming, doesn't like it when I talk about being satisfied or not being satisfied. Mum's the only one I don't lie to out of politeness. She wonders where I got my stuck-up ideas, takes it like a slap in the face. What's good enough for her, and all that. Perhaps she knows I'll only be disappointed when I don't get anywhere so is trying to save me the hurt, convince me that it'd be far better to accept what I've already got, even if it's not too much.

I'm scared, don't feel ready or properly prepared to get on with the things that matter. Experience is a horrible thought. I don't want to have to make my own decisions in case I get it wrong and make a fool of myself in front of everyone. Gran says that Mum – only because she loved me so much and because she thought I was going to be her only child – cradled me too fiercely. She didn't want me to have to cope with the consequence of mistakes so she never let me make any, i.e. I never learned. Not that I want to agree with anything that puts Mum down, though sometimes I do wonder why I feel so ignorant. I can't even talk to more than one person at a time – fluff my words. Feels like I don't fit in, like I offend people by just being me. And I creep to people that I don't even like. After, I wonder what horrid things they're saying about me.

I'm not sure if the majority of guests didn't know that Mum was pregnant, or if they thought it best not to mention it. I was real worried about when she'd have her baby, Bob's baby. Then, they'd be a family, I'd be on the outside. Some things are bound to come with a kid, I could imagine all the years of crying, colds, coughs, croup, constipation. Messy noses, messy bums. Like a balloon was going to pop and change the quiet, the people, the warm things in my world. Would Mum have time for me? Was it fair to expect her to? If not I'd have to rely on myself but I couldn't, because I'd be nothing without her.

Mum's always done her best for me. I wanted to say to her 'please keep me safe', but somehow she'd take it the worst possible way so I never said it. She's always apologising to people unnecessarily. I'm never going to apologise. Not ever.

When I went back inside, Stu had just finished off the 'when Bob got smashed and lost his dentures down the bog' story. Nobody questioned my absence. Probably thought I was sulking.

The happy couple didn't have a honeymoon, that evening was just like any other. Except it was much more 'hand-up-shirt-and-snoggy' on the sofa.

'How did I look, Bob?'

'All right.'

'Did you like the dress then?'

'Um. All right. How much did that set you back?'

'Shall we do something special tomorrow, Bob?'

'Why?'

'To celebrate, silly.'

'Like what?'

'Well, I don't know.'

'No. Not worth it. Probably rain anyway.'

'No. Perhaps you're right.'

I wanted to punch them both. When I was small and felt upset, I'd shut myself in the airing cupboard. It was just right to nestle between the tank and a pile of fresh linen, that special, clean smell. Too big now, and I'd feel dumb. Hadn't done it for ages, not since I started my periods – stayed in there all day then. Too stunned to come out. Mum had come looking for me, when she found me she grinned and was kind of 'pleasant'. I felt stupid and didn't want to talk about it, just do what had to be done but Mum seemed pleased, proud almost, and kept going on about it. Sometimes she tells people about, that day.

'And d'you know she was in the airing cupboard at the top of the stairs – after all that searching, all that worry. And guess what. She'd actually 'come on' for the very first time. Poor little mite. Ahhh, what a day.'

It wasn't that I hadn't been warned about this dreadful occurrence. I just thought that I'd be saved for some unknown reason, it wouldn't happen until *I* wanted it to. Though I'd certainly not considered what it'd be like to have great big wads of cotton wool shoved down my knickers and was wholly unimpressed.

The day after the wedding I took our flowers and put them on Grandad's grave. When I'm feeling self-pity inside, I think of all the times I've been horrible to people. Sometimes the things I do, or have done, are disguised as another meaning, but in the end it results in hurt and so I have to punish myself. I enjoy punishing myself. Grandad came round to our house a lot. I liked him. He had a funny accent and a strawberry nose, never complained about anything. Still, *they* used to say that he was a miserable old git, but I bet he was conjuring up poetry in his mind – I bet anything he was. He'd sit outside in the garden if he could – when the weather was good enough, always knew where to find him. Really admired the garden, the bright colours. Dad was into all that y'see, kept it right up together, weedless. Grandad only had an allotment and everybody wants the next best thing upwards.

I love faces that never try to hide anything, hills and valleys, orange peel textures. Faces that tell stories. I used to feel responsible for him in a way, seemed as if the others used to treat him as if he didn't count anymore, but to me it was like he was floating away unnoticed and would soon be gone for ever. All his tales would be lost. I'd beg him to show me the veins on his legs. I liked to try his cap, always temporarily removed in the garden, as a sign of respect he said. The two-tone silk lining would darken if I dribbled on it. Once the idea had come to me that if I stood behind him as he sat there, I could spit down on to his white hair without him ever guessing what it was, where it came from. For an instant it had been so terribly funny. It worked. Ran down over his brow, off to the side of his face. But then I saw a tear roll to his cheek. He had guessed, must have felt so old and useless. Two streams then, one of sadness, one of shame. The globule of saliva fell to his chin, he wiped it with one hand and looked away. I wanted to cry too, wanted to hug him, tell him it was all right, that I didn't mean it, was sorry, so sorry. Tell him that I loved him. Didn't have the guts; instead mouthed, 'silly old fool', and ran away. I hated it. Like I hate being cruel to people now, making them feel helpless, yet at the same time it makes me feel good, better.

On the way back home I bumped into Sophie, a friend, my best friend. I was cold from the churchyard, she asked me to her place for a drink and something to eat. Their house is far grander than ours, I hoped that people would see me walking up the drive and think that I lived there and not her. She'd spent the whole weekend playing Monopoly. Except her mum had taken her out to buy new shoes at some stage. Black ones, leather with slim heels and pointed toes. She walked in them for me. Sophie doesn't walk though, she glides, saunters, struts, but never just walks. She let me try them on, then put them alongside her other pairs, all in a row, standing to attention like they were too frightened to show any signs of wear. Sophie's room – it cuddles you as you step into it – the sheepskin rug tickles up between your toes, smiles and says 'Hello'.

I told her about the wedding, about the baby – hadn't said anything about that before because Mum had intended to keep it a secret until after they were married, even though she'd spread the news herself and asked of each person 'Don't say anything to anyone else – you know how people talk'. If Sophie already knew, then she gave a admirable performance.

'Pregnant! God! I'd just hate it, if mine had a . . . Oh, that's really terrible. Don't you mind?'

'A bit. Not sure yet.'

'I bet mine haven't done IT for years. I mean, I can't imagine. It's awful for you – just think what it'll be like. Was it on purpose?'

' 'Spect so.'

'What does she want a baby for? If you ask me it's pretty irresponsible at her age.'

'She's only thirty-six. And I think he wanted one, mostly. And the Pill made her fat.'

'Mine doesn't agree with the Pill, not right to interfere with your body, with nature. She tell you that she was taking it?'

'Yeah, but only when I happened to be there and she

got one stuck in her throat. I had to fetch a glass of water so's she could wash it down.'

'In her throat! You're kidding me? She didn't swallow them surely!'

'Course. Why?'

'Fool! You're meant to stick them up. You know. Inside. Silly fool! It's to form a barrier, when there's enough of them it stops anything getting through. You know. How else is it going to have any effect? God knows what damage she's done.'

I couldn't argue, thought that perhaps there might be two different sorts. I liked the subject though, and Sophie seemed to know so much more than I did.

'You don't think yours do it any more then?'

'No. Never even seen them kiss. Anyway nearly everyone's stopped by *their* age! And I'm glad.'

'It's got it all in my dictionary – the one I had for Christmas – penis, sod, *masturbate* . . . '

'Yuk!'

'Have you ever wondered what it's like?'

'Certainly not!'

'Nor have I. But what do you think it's like?'

Sophie keeps quiet when she can't think up the right answer. I was determined to talk about IT, things.

'It's got it in the dictionary, but doesn't say exactly how to do it.'

'Don't you know anything?'

'Well, I do *know*, what I mean is, it doesn't say, and some people might not know.'

'Why don't you do it if you want to find out what it's like. But it's only for men really.'

'Why don't you? You scared?'

'Infant. *Nothing* scares me.'

'I dare you then.'

'I dare you in return.'

'Okay. We both will. Tonight.'

'Right.'

'Right.'

Sophie's Mum had made a nice dinner, something called ratatouille. They made out that there were real rats in it to start with but I could see there weren't any. I couldn't imagine Sophie's mum doing sex either, she doesn't even wear mascara.

And I didn't try it, you know, beginning with m . . . I said I did. Sophie said she did too. We agreed that it was easy and no big deal, though we couldn't really describe it. It was a relief that she didn't keep on about it – just in case she really had.

Before long, our house was riddled with nappies and nappy-linked chat. Mum gave up smoking and drinking, or tried. At first it put her in terrible moods. I gave up trying to fool myself. Couldn't get it out of my mind. It must be partly my fault. I should have run, screamed, got away. I should have told somebody. I just let him do it, like it was nothing, nothing new.

Rape, to take by force.

Prostitute, to offer one's body for sexual intercourse in return for payment.

Incest, sexual contact between persons too closely related to marry, or between a child and an adult in a position of trust.

I got down on my knees.

'Please, God, I didn't want to give in. I couldn't help it, if you make it happen again then I'll show you, show you how it was. Please don't let anybody find out.'

You know, the girls in my class always make jokes about sex. Some boast, say they've done it loads of times, tell how lovely it is. I can't stand the way they talk in case they try to involve me – be obvious up against their dreamy lies, obvious that I *had*, whereas they *hadn't*. They laugh about virgins. Just like they'd laugh to know that I didn't enjoy it. Just like one day they'll pretend to enjoy it. They'd love to know about me – I'd be a hero. They'd ask me then – about what it's like, if it hurts much to start with. I hate great big loud girls that push and crush. If anyone was to find out I could be taken away, from home, from Mum. Better to fill every day with nothing if that's the only option. Up to me to take care of myself.

Mum called her bump (which was still pretty much non-existent) 'M', an abbreviation for Michael or Michelle. She constantly talked of 'scan' and 'epidural'. All my old baby clothes came down from the loft and I was mad – they were mine, I wanted to keep them. She washed and pressed them, ready for the big event. She even bought a film for her camera when there were still five or six months to go. The huge bellied smocks were out and in full use, bottles were lined up on the window ledge, baby shampoo and talc were in the bathroom cabinet. Gran knitted a hundred pairs of booties and a thousand cardigans – all the same design.

And Bob found work, just like Mum promised he would. Only part-time, behind a bar, but it was a real job with real money. He still drew his dole, Mum didn't like that too much but it didn't stop her from spending it. No matter what happened, she always made sure there was enough left over to buy Chinese take-away every Saturday night. I looked forward to it – we'd stay up late, playing Consequences usually. Anything that's not funny was banned – whoever got serious first had to pay a penalty, go out in the road and sing a song or do cartwheels. I love it when you've laughed for so long that you can't remember what it was about. Bob and Mum were happy together. She was different, all excited and bubbly, until she got tired. Then she was a right pain and best avoided. I tried to help out as much as I could. She paid me for giving her a hand around the house (top secret), I never asked for the money but always hoped I'd get some and that she wouldn't forget. With the savings, I bought a rabbit from a place that breeds them especially to eat. Could say that I saved his life, could say it without doubt. Called him Rover just to be awkward, though later I changed it to Adolf having dreamt that my bunny was in fact the reincarnation of Adolf Hitler. I built a run so as he wouldn't escape and a little box for him to sleep in, padded it out with hay. It wasn't very good. I could really talk to him. And I did, never answered back, passed judgment or got fed up with the same old things. I could tell him about how they all think they're so smart. Think that what they've got is all there is. That really they've got absolutely nothing. They don't believe that someone like me has an inside, one that they don't know about. They think they know everything. But some things, they just don't want to know about. That doesn't make those things go away. They say they care. They don't know what care means. Care means talk, care means listen, as equals. Nothing to do with 'a laugh', some sweets or new clothes. Things mean nothing in a place where there's no interest in people. I want to break 'things' up, then there'd be little left to do except find out about one another.

The day I got Adolf, brought him home, nobody had time to meet him, say hello even. Big trouble going on. I decided that I'd like to come back as a different creature. A snake with scarlet fangs. Didn't want to be a human.

Gran, in her total state of 'confusion', had had a small 'accident', a 'mishap'. Got caught shop-lifting. Wasn't any surprise to me, I knew she'd been doing it for as long as I could remember so the law of averages said that one day she'd be found out. Made it look simple though. She'd put her own bag next to the wire basket, on the same arm, then it'd be 'one for you, one for me, one for you, two for me'. Usually she went for things like deodorant or soaps, cosmetic things – just the right size to handle, slipped through her hands with such ease and confidence. This time it'd been a box of crackers for cheese, a bit too big to glide through her fingers unnoticed. About the size of a small loaf. She doesn't even like them. Mum fetched her from the Co-op with Bob, borrowed next door's car. Brought her back to our house, straight into the kitchen for an emergency brew.

'Yes, but did you do it, Mum?'

'I s'pose I must have if that's what they're saying?'

'Mum! Did you do it *on purpose*?'

'I'm old, love.'

'MUM!'

Bob interrupted where he wasn't required.

'Everyone nicks something sometime.'

'Are you calling my mother a bloody thief, Bob?'

'Well, it's true.'

'Because if you are, if you're calling *my* mother . . . '

'I'm not. I said everybody picks something up now and again, human nature – I don't care who they are or what they say, we all like something for nothin' if we can get away with it.'

'Bob, you don't seem to understand – Mum might be prosecuted.'

'Won't come to much. A fine. No loss to these big concerns anyway.'

'*Bob*!'

Gran didn't seem too bothered, put her 'dithering and senile' act on to escape further interrogation. I wondered if it'd be in the paper but didn't dare to mention it. We sat back, let Mum and Bob argue over it. Think Gran was glad to have me there, someone to sneak off with. It was quieter in the front room on our own, we closed the door, warmed by the 'lectric fire like always. Her hands were weaving over each other, I could hear the roughness snag, she picked her nails in turn.

'Gran . . .'

Her sigh pleaded, Oh don't you start . . .

'What, love?'

'I read this thing the other day. It said that, well, prostitutes aren't only women who do things for money, it can mean other stuff too . . .'

'What you talking about?'

'Well, I just wondered what you thought . . . '

'Well stop wonderin', fillin' your head with such rubbish.'

'It's only something I read. In a book. A magazine. It said that when people say they've been well, raped, sometimes, well, you know, it's their own fault, they wouldn't have let it happen if they hadn't wanted it to, so really they're like a prostitute . . . '

'Stop drivelling. Don't know what bloody books you read.'

'But could that be true?'

'In a way.'

'How?'

'Well, they mean that some women flaunt themselves, like a bloody bitch on heat, actually say no but obviously really mean yes. Change their minds afterwards, that sort of thing.'

'So it could be true?'

'Not like a prostitute. I wouldn't say that. Just get what they asked for – it's no good coming on strong to a man and then later expecting him to walk away.'

I thought it over for a long time. Couldn't decide whether or not I'd egged Bob on. By not fighting back hard enough. Perhaps he thought I wanted it to happen. Perhaps the reason I couldn't shout out or fight was because really, deep down, I did want it to happen. I know him. Know him well. Mum's man, someone she trusts. How could it be right to say that he was wrong and not me? He never talked to me about it. Went on ignoring me like always. Everything just the same as always. Everything normal. I didn't even do anything to try and make sure it didn't happen again. Nothing. Not like a prostitute though. I haven't got that much courage. I'd be proud to think I was so brave.

I told Sophie all about Gran's shop-lifting, in the yard at breaktime. She said it'd be best to believe that Gran had picked the biscuits up from the shelf, then wandered around the shop and forgot she had hold of them. It's happened to loads of people apparently, especially Gran types, getting on a bit, muddled minds and all that. But, if it came to the newspaper and the kids at school said anything, she'd back me up in the fabrication that Gran wasn't really my Gran. No relation at all, just a name I'd always called her, like Jane or Sheila (any surname similarities were purely a coincidence). An old lady, lonely, that I'd befriended out of kindness, felt sorry for her living on her own, no friends or family. Well, I couldn't come up with anything better. But on the second issue she hadn't been so helpful.

'Where did you read that?'

'Can't remember. Just in a book. One of Mum's books.'

'What sort of book? Bring it to school, let me read it.'

'Can't, think she's thrown it out. Can't find it.'

'Promise you'll look.'

'I'll look.'

'And it said that when a girl's raped it might be her fault?'

'Yeah.'

'Um. Well. Of course they're right. Sometimes. I saw a documentary once. Some women, rough ones, actually enjoy violence – it didn't say that on TV but that's what Dad says. And there's lots of different ways of flirting. Like you can say suggestive things, say nothing at all, sort of tantalise. You can walk sexily or . . .'

'What should you do then, to get rid of them?'

'Easy. Say, "*No way*", and run, you'd make loads of noise to draw attention to yourself, attract someone who could help you.'

'What if they grabbed you and no one was around?'

'Throw something in their eyes to sting, blind them for a few seconds so you could get away, perfume, pepper.'

'And if you didn't have anything to throw?'

'Kick them between the legs of course. I'd never let them do it, not ever. I'd fight until I dropped down dead. I'd find strength from inside that I never knew was there. Fight to kill. No one would *ever* do that to me.'

But Sophie couldn't know, not really. Nor Gran for that matter, she's ancient, unreliable. Experience means more than anything else. I reckoned Mum'd know more about reality. Mum's lived while all most people do is to make plans to live. They haven't begun, she's roared through the lot, twice over. Mum's a 'yes' or 'no' woman. It wasn't difficult to find the right moment – we ended up at the sink together every night.

'Fancy madam Sophie having a book like that. Miss prim and proper, I am surprised. Thought that type of thing'd be too adventurous for her eyes.'

'Only a magazine. Had loads of other things in it too.'

'Rape. Well, I don't know, love. When someone, you know, when you don't want him to, if you ask me, he should be castrated.'

'Castrated?'

'Have his whatsits chopped off. Bet they do just that in some countries. We're too bloody soft here.'

'So it's the man's fault?'

'Oh, definitely. Definitely the man's fault, love. But, then, in some cases how can you be sure the woman's not lying to get back at him for something else – or because she wished she hadn't done it?'

Oh shit, I don't know. Still don't know. Shouldn't I feel sick, or numb, or become hysterical each time he looks at me?

Three

My body's all messy compared to Sophie's. I'm still a gawky kid and she's elegant and graceful. Long, like a dancer. Against her I feel like an imbecile. Once, even Bob remarked on how pretty she'd got – reckons her parents are in 'for a load of trouble'. Since working at the pub he'd started picking up so-called jokes, throw-away one-liners, things that weren't the slightest bit funny. Mum lost all patience.

'Oral sex is a matter of taste.'

'What?'

'Oral sex is a matter of taste – get it?'

'Oh. Yeah.'

'You're not laughing.'

'No.'

'Nuclear arms? Bomb the bastards. The bad news is I'm gay. The good news is I'll probably be wiped out by AIDS soon.'

'Bob. Piss off.'

With the extra money coming in, Mum saved up and managed to get a pram. A posh one, burgundy cord, all padded inside. When the baby got too big it'd convert into a pushchair. There was a matching canopy to be bought but she couldn't afford it, much too expensive. Pleased all the same, real craftsmanship that pram – so Mum said. The spare room officially became M's room. Hadn't been done out or anything – looked just the same – except for the piles of stuff Mum'd either bought or been given. There was a lemon potty, a second-hand cot still in pieces, a couple of shawls volunteered by the dreaded Ada, crochet of a fashion, a huge fawn teddy with bulging eyes in flourescent lime plastic, sent over by Stu's Julie. Oh, and sanitary towels galore, the modern sort. I liked the ones with loops better, made good hammocks for Sindy and Action Man when they were in the jungle. Bob reckoned he'd watch Mum give birth. Her suggestion so that makes it all right. I suppose. I felt a bit left out but tried not to show it.

Had a nice surprise one Sunday morning. Woke up to a load of snow. Mountains of it. Didn't look real from the bedroom window, more like heaps of salt or chalk. Sophie and me had a great time, just mucking around while the fogies stayed in and discussed the prevention of frozen and burst pipes. Our lavatory got blocked – don't know if it had anything to do with the weather or not, only that we couldn't use it properly for a few days. Then everyone who called at the house needed the loo desperately. Mum'd say, 'Toilet? Yes, of course,' then stretch her mouth and exaggerate, 'but don't flush,' in no more than a whisper, like it was rude. As soon as they were out of earshot she'd mumble, 'Bloody hell, who went last? How bad was it?'

I found a piece of corrugated iron out the back, we used it as a sleigh. It went so fast, we had to jump off and hope we landed somewhere not too painful, there was no way of stopping it. You should see the snow outfit that Sophie's got. White and quilted, scarf and gloves somehow attached, piped in cerise. Her dad bought it for her when she went ski-ing with the school last year, Switzerland I think, or Italy. She said that she preferred it at my place because we could do more or less as we wanted, at her's you're always a bit worried about doing something wrong, spoiling something.

I think Sophie'll be a prefect. Or even Head Girl. Her

dad says she'll go to university. Not any old place – a good one. She's quite interested in animals and might be a vet. They've got loads of books at their house (the red sort with gold writing on the outside), she was able to give me several tips on caring for Adolf. She's so clever, knows about everything – the Conservative Party, trade unions, the money market, Britain's defence system, the history of the monarchy, the history of George Michael. Her dad talks with her a lot, explains things, tells her what he thinks and why she's got to think the same. If she's not a vet, she might be a scientist instead. Myself, I'd like to be a cook. Good at cooking, well, I'm not too bad. I've got seven books on the subject, all mine, not Mum's, so I reckon I've got a head start on some people. One of them is devoted to puddings and nothing else. The last thing I made was scones, trouble was they stuck to the table, all gooey like neutral phlegm. I had to scrape the mixture up together and flop it into roundish shapes before baking them. So perhaps I'll be a cook in a place where they don't serve scones.

Mum's a romantic I think, she wanted to make each complete month of marriage something special, like a proper anniversary. The first, she made spaghetti bolognese with cheese. On the second she bought a heart-shaped tin and made a chocolate sponge, from a box, not a real one. It was good, though a piece of the side broke off as she tried to free it from the sticky, non-stick base. Didn't really matter – we covered it in icing to hide the imperfections. Put smarties on the top – I love orange smarties. I 'spect she would have done herself up a bit if it wasn't for being pregnant.

We waited for Bob in the kitchen.

'Look – you're walking straight past it!'

'Past what?'

'The cake.'

'What's that for?'

'Guess.'

'How should I know?'

'Guess.'

'Not bothered if you're not gunna tell me . . . .'

'What happened two months ago today? Now there's a clue!'

'What?'

'Think!'

'Oh, that. Soppy cow.'

She hugged him while he read the newspaper. He doesn't like chocolate cake, or so he said – I'm sure I've seen him guts it back before. I only had one slice in case it's true that chocolate gives you spots. Mum polished off the rest over a couple of days.

Later that night, Bob went and collected the car he'd been harping on about. A Ford Cortina, metallic brown. Mum was mad at first. He pointed out the baby seat in the back and she fell for it, the blow immediately softened. He might be an idiot but he's no fool.

I'd say we'd swapped places, me and Mum. I'd always been all right, but wasn't any more. She'd believed that nothing was ever going to work out for her again, and here she was, happy, full stop. We never seemed to smile at the same times, meet in the middle. Never felt the same way. It would've been much better if I wasn't there, better for them. Think Mum thought that sometimes. Know Bob did. I'd catch her looking across at me as they snuggled up in the chair. When I looked back, she'd pretend she wasn't doing it and just clear her throat or wipe her nose to give her something else to do. Her expression would say it though, 'Well, what are *you* hanging around for?' Bob wasn't as tactful, he admitted he'd be glad when I was old enough to leave home so's they could have the place to themselves.

I hated to way Mum acted like a little servant, a little

trotting dog. I hated his hands on my mother's skin, didn't want him to touch her like he did. Not touch, it wasn't that, more paw. When he was watching telly, she'd lie across him, gazing at his face, all this admiration pouring from her. When he laughed, she laughed. When he was hungry, she was hungry. When he said 'bed', then bed it was. This man from out of nowhere, just walks in, takes my mother from me, takes me from myself. I wanted her, I wanted me. But she was always on *his* side, had to agree with *him*, *he* took priority. He'd tell me to do things, make the tea, switch the telly over, get his fags and she backed him up. And he'd clip my ear. This man, not even my real father, comes into *my* house and it's fine if he feels like swiping me with the back of his hand.

Sometimes I wish I was an aeroplane, indestructable, zooming around the sky, crashing into people and places that I don't like. I'd bounce off, like rubber, ready to start again. No one would dare touch me, they'd come close to look but not so close that I could push them into a swamp. I'd be rage. They'd be heaped all around me, trying to stay calm as the ground shook. Then they'd limp away till next time, until I came back.

Or a vulture. I could be a vulture, peck at people's make-believe armour, claw through the gaps and pull it away, down, smashed. They'd try and cover their nudeness with inventions of ignorance. I'd show them a mirror, one with no reflection. Kings would turn to liquid. Liquid that couldn't even make things damp, only trickle away. Having strength means you don't get crushed. And I'll get strength.

On my fourteenth birthday, not unusually, plans to celebrate were last minute. I don't mind that. If it's all arranged in advance you tend to build your hopes up only to be let down. Gran came round but didn't have a present. Bob said, behind her back, that it was just as well – didn't want to get into any bother for receiving stolen goods. He'd taken to calling her Granny Biggs. I must say that when she admitted to bearing no big fat gift, I'd called her a bloody convict in my head. The only things I've ever nicked are fags from Mum and three quid from Bob's trouser pocket when he'd left them out for washing without checking for cash. He can't talk, nor her, what about our fridge, our video.

Sophie (she stole an ice cream sundae from their freezer once), gave me a writing set in different shades of blue, and a nice pen. Mum gave me a fiver to buy whatever I wanted. Dad phoned.

'All right, love?'

'Yeah, thanks.'

'Happy birthday.'

'Thanks.'

'What you doin?'

'Nothing much. Gran's round.'

'Oh, that's nice.'

'Yeah.'

'Your card's in the post – I was a bit late. You know what I'm like for remembering things.'

'Yeah, that's okay.'

'Had many presents?'

'A few.'

'Good.'

Silence.

'Well, now I know everything's goin' all right then. Haven't bought you anythin' yet, but I will do, Saturday.'

'Okay.'

'See you soon then, take care.'

'Bye, Dad, see you.'

He wouldn't get me anything, the card wouldn't be in the post, I wouldn't see him.

Mum wanted to know the ins and outs as we laid the table.

'Who was that?'

'Dad.'

'What did *he* want?'

'Just to say happy birthday.'

'What did he say then?'

'Well, just happy birthday.'

'Has he bought you anything?'

'Not yet.'

'Bloody wouldn't have would he? Thinks nothin' of you.'

'He said he was getting something at the weekend.'

'What was wrong with last weekend, yesterday, today? His own bloody daughter. Not even a lousy card. Thinks sod all about anybody except himself – it's worth considering that when he comes creeping round. Bob's more of a father to you than he's ever been.'

Silence.

'He needn't think he'll win you over with some extravagent I-don't-know-what in three weeks' time. Not that he will bring anything, doesn't give a damn. It's me he's getting at. Better not set foot inside this door.'

I wanted to scream. Shut up, go away, leave me alone. I don't need this, don't need it one bit. Don't want to know that he doesn't care, doesn't want me. He does. In his own way. Bob and Gran chirped up in unison as they came into the front room from the kitchen, ready to start on the food, and on Dad – eavesdroppers.

'What did *he* want?'

'To wish her a happy birthday.'

Bob banged his hand on the table, made it shake.

'Get my fist down 'is throat if I ever see 'im again.'

'Bob.'

'Bloody will.'

Gran took Bob's view.

'Don't defend that maniac, Stephanie, nothin' but trouble.'

Mum didn't answer, she knew it could blow up into a full-scale battle at any second. The subject was temporarily dropped, even if the atmosphere wasn't. I felt sorry for Sophie. She'd perched on the edge of her seat all the time, looking around at nothing, saying nothing. She wasn't used to scenes, it's not like that at her house. One egg sandwich and topic resumed by the semi-resident criminal.

'What *exactly* did he say then?'

'Who?'

'How many phone calls have you had today? Who d'you think?'

'He said *happy birthday*.'

Bob's turn.

'Took 'im a long time to say two words. Wanted to know about your mother I s'pose?'

Mum asked Sophie if her cake was nice and what type of sandwiches she liked the best.

'Bloody long time to say two words.'

I could see how nervous Mum was, dead scared of him, that he'd start something big. She suggested that Sophie and me went out for a walk. Happened to be a blizzard outside. We went to Sophie's and had hot chocolate by the open fireside. It was lovely, the best part of my day. Her mum and dad chat about what they've done during the day, about all sorts of things. Not in raised voices, being annoyed, they talk like me and Sophie do – as if they're friends as well as being married to each other. They said that I could go around there as often as I liked.

Sophie's mum is not the same as my mum. Quiet like a little sparrow in its nest. Bet she'd never wear her slippers to the shops. Or call out to someone across the road. Bet she never has a really good time though, or does much hard work. I s'pose work isn't everything, so long as you're happy. Might take more guts to admit that you actually don't like hard work, why work when you can not work, so long as you've got money and friends. I quite liked her once I got to know her better. I'd thought she was weird to start but I think she's shy. Mum's never liked her, nor Gran. Bob does impressions of the way she talks, so I'd guess he's not too impressed either. Her voice isn't posh, ordinary really, but *soft*, without any dialect. She asked *me* questions. Didn't poke fun at the answers I gave. Or say that she knew better. Made me feel important, like I mattered, what *I* thought meant something. Gave me a lift home – wouldn't hear that I'd be fine to walk. I felt proud to be fourteen, it's almost adult really.

The pram was in the hall. Mum was in the kitchen. Bob was out. Gran had gone home. A row. He'd spotted the new pram for the first time and it'd been niggling him – Dad's phone call was an excuse to get started. Said the pram was horrible, as well as being totally unnecessary. Hates it if she buys anything without consulting him before going ahead. Said she had to take it back to the shop, get the money back. She was worried – they don't usually exchange goods for cash, only a credit note. Worried about Bob's temper.

It's as though Bob really did want this baby – until it was real. Then he couldn't stand it because she had to devote everything to it. Her body, her future, her money, her time. Like all of a sudden it was nothing to do with him, he wasn't part of it, it was *her* baby. Poor old M. Best off staying in the warm.

Then, something stupid happened. Something stupid to a stupid person. Sounds pathetic because that's what it is.

Sophie was playing for the school hockey team, first time she'd been picked. Asked me along to witness her debut and to give her some encouragement. It was an awful day right from the start. The edge of the pitch is an isolated place to be, especially when you don't know the rules of the game. I tried my hardest to be noticeably active, cheering when our side got the ball, booing when the other team got it. We lost, but only due to injuries Sophie said.

After the match, I went with her, back to the changing rooms. The usual big rush, everybody running off to catch buses or lifts home. We didn't have to. Took our time, talked about the other girls, how silly they were, what childish things they'd said or been doing. Sophie showered.

And just for one moment, one fraction of a second. How she was, she *made me* want to reach out and touch her, hold on to her, tell her what she meant to me, as my friend, my only friend in the whole wide world. I got this feeling, a sort of ache that needed to be relieved. A nice ache, so nice that I didn't want it to go away too soon.

Right the way home she kept pestering me, asking me what was wrong, why I'd gone moody and wouldn't talk to her properly. I was trying not to like her so much.

That night I ate a chunk of soap to make myself sick, the one way I'd be sure to get out of the next day's school would be on the pretence of some chronic stomach disorder. Wouldn't last for ever, but I'd be saved from Sophie, from me, until I could think of something more permanent to stop my ache from coming back.

Mum noticed how down I was. She'd blame World War Three on someone's heavy period or, 'the curse', 'aunty', as she insists on calling it most of the time. I wanted to tell her. I don't know what I wanted to tell her. But bawl something obscene that'd shock her into taking me seriously. Never did. Never have. Just sit there all tongue-tied, a little girl. Mum was doing our washing, by hand mostly but the rumble of the twin tub was always there in the background. She still used the big wooden tongs that I could remember from a hundred years before. Still struggled on, hauling the wet stuff out and into the spinner, burning her hand or arm on the steam. Everything in our kitchen is chipped. Everything that was white is nicotine yellow. Except the new wall tin-opener. I don't like formica. I don't like the way that washing up bowls go all flaky when they're old, when the plastic starts to peel. I don't like tea-strainers or rainbow cosies. I don't like chaos, though never do much to avoid it.

Food is one of the most consoling things there is. I stuffed at least one packet of coconut cookies, sitting there, quiet, just watching Mum work. We've always got biscuits if there's nothing else. Love custard creams and chocolate bourbons. Once, Mum had to choose between a new pair of tights and a packet of bourbons. Guess which she chose? The bourbons. Made do with old holey tights, they'd be okay, so long as our tums were content. She's always worn the same shades of tights, dark grey for special occasions, tan for ordinary. Unless it's summer and she can go without. I look forward to the feel of putting on brand-new tights, so does Mum.

The soap trick didn't actually make me sick, I couldn't bring myself to eat any more – it'd scalded the tip of my tounge down to my belly. Mum thought I looked peeky though (I'd rubbed talcum powder into my face), and said that I could stay home from school – well, she wasn't to know. I lay in bed until Bob'd gone to work and Mum out for the day (pram first, then clinic). Surfaced at about twelve.

There was a note for Bob on the sideboard to say that if she was late home, he wasn't to worry about cooking, she'd bring something from the take-away. She'd signed it with about six million kisses in the shape of an 'S', he'd added, 'does this S stand for screw?' The difference between me and Mum is that she'd read it and laugh, say what a lad he was. Whereas I'd not have written the stupid note in the first place – he's not helpless – and if I had, I'd feel really disappointed.

In the afternoon I tried on some of Mum's clothes and shoes. When I'm in school uniform, I look like a baby, yet when I put something more, you know, older on, I look different. In a pencil skirt I almost look – no I don't. I curled my hair with the tongs, clipped it up on one side. Would've felt hideous if anyone'd seen, even though I quite liked it. At this age, people think it's all just playing, sometimes it is, but other times it's not. A few girls at school do themselves up and look nice, but I'd be scared of looking like a little kid trying to be a grown up and not pulling it off.

Mum's room, it's lovely, but an absolute tip. Cleanser, eye make-up remover, nail varnish, beads, earrings, tissues, foundation cream, blusher, mascara, radio, knickers, hair dye, perfume. The bed is rarely made, the brown duvet flops at the bottom. You can never see yourself clearly in the mirror, always coated with layers of hair spray. There's mugs, ashtrays, sweet wrappers, the lot, it's all there somewhere, even though she cleans it two or three times a week.

At night Mum puts soft rollers in her hair, looks ridiculous. Fixes a kind of bath cap thing over the top. I like those bedrooms you get on telly best of all. They've never seen a hair roller. White fittings, white carpet, no mess. That's what I want. Or proper wood. Not fake like Mum's. Her units have bowed at the sides and the shelves collapse, fall straight through to the bottom in a pile.

When Mum's out I go into her room to be with her, feel close to her. It's like her room really is her, has her smell, her things – everything that makes her into the person she is. She wouldn't like me to touch anything, I just breathe her in and feel safe. There's none of him in there even though it's his room too. When it suits him.

Later on I got bored, watched telly. There was a programme on about war. Not any one war in particular, just war. Some of the soldiers were teenagers, not much older than me. People might think they're terrible. Sometimes, I feel like I could kill. Don't care who it is, the same as they don't. The picture kept flicking from one dead body to another. I wanted to smash the screen, smash the room, smash the street. I cried with the cries of the children, the roar of the gunfire, the anger of the soliders. Sophie said I was mental when she found me bawling. Wouldn't tell her what was up. Couldn't look at her face. She'd waltzed in, five past four, thrust an envelope into my hands. I didn't know, but I thought it was meant for me. It wasn't. Inside was a pathetic little card with kittens on. Scrawled in purple felt-tip pen, 'To Soph, from an admirer. Guess who?' Soph! Nobody *ever* called her things like *that*! She had a proudness about her.

'Load of crap.'

'Just because you've never had a love letter.'

'Love letter? Call that a love letter?'

'Even Bob's sort of had one from your mum – over there on the sideboard.'

'Don't you read *that*. It's private. And don't be immature – doesn't suit you.'

'Nothing immature about love letters. If there was your mum wouldn't send them would she?'

'But she is immature.'

How I didn't rip it up. Fucking notes. I felt betrayed, wanted her to be all mine, enough mine to be able to confide in her. Sharing means splitting, means weaker, means less important, less faithful.

Why has there got to be sex? I don't want to know about it. Maybe I stick my nose into other people's business, maybe they could be more considerate. My mum, his wife. Our lover. It's like he hadn't been around long enough to do so much to us, mean so much to her, wipe me away. But she loves him, I 'spect that's what it's like when you're in love. Not her fault. I didn't know what was happening with them, with my aching. Always pretended to know it all. Can remember one dreaded confrontation with Mum, equally uncomfortable for the pair of us. Parents aren't any good at explaining real things. It's like they have to admit to doing something really naughty. Everything's SEX. Whenever Mum had tried to explain anything she'd acted like a girl guide. Definitely thinks I don't need to know *all* yet. The only time she's ever talked seriously about it . . .

'Love. I know you know about, well, periods. But what about having a baby and all that?'

'Yeah. I know.'

'You certain?'

'Yeah.'

'Everything?'

'Yeah.'

'How d'you know?'

'Just do. From school.'

'Oh. That's all right then.'

There was something, but I had to turn away from her.

'What about oral sex?'

Her voice was thin, like renewed panic after relief.

'What about it?'

'Well. What is it?'
'Kissing.'
'Kissing?'
'Yes, kissing?'
'Is that all?'
'Yes.'
'Why don't people just say "kissing" then?'
'Well. *Kissing*, you know.'
I did, but didn't.
After that, it was up to the desks.
'Dave's got eight inches when it's hard'
'Julie's up the stick'
Mum used to have some books that could be quite good for that type of thing, somebody Robbins. I read little snatches in secret but most of the time they raised more questions than they answered. Went on about cats with loads of tails – rubbish. I found some disgusting magazines too, on *his* side of the mattress. At least they showed me where everything was, is.

Mum *said* I could ask about anything, any time, made it all sound so simple.

'Now, if you don't understand, ask. Me or Bob, nothing to get embarrassed over.'

Why not just us, that's what I want to know, why's Bob got to be involved all the time? Christ, what I could tell her about precious Bob. The disease, the tumor I'd asked for, in my head, gnawing. Course, I'll get over it – that's what they'd all say. Nothing *too* bad, just spilling out of me as I breathe, that's all, nothing much. Asleep, awake, makes no difference to me, it grows and swells. God, if she knew, she'd die. And I do love her, that woman. She'd never come through it. He'd still be her husband, but I'd never be her child again.

I wondered when they'd stop doing it. Thought it might hurt the baby as time went on. Thought that if he couldn't do it with her, then he might want to do it with me again. Once, when I got out of bed in the night, I heard them arguing about it. Not much, just,

'I'm worn out . . . '

'Lesbian.'

He thinks that's the ultimate insult. Bob hates lesbians. That's what he'd call me if he thought I could feel anything for someone other than a male, including what I feel for Mum. I'm not one but if I were, he'd turn something special into something dirty. That's what people like him enjoy doing. That's why I'd keep it a secret, or p'raps I wouldn't. I don't know what lesbians do, together. Only that love is love, whoever it's between, if only for a day. And love is better than hate. He says that lesbians are ill, could be cured, just haven't found a good man yet, that he could put them on the right track. He hates men ones even more. Reckons if they can't be normal they should be hanged. He never uses the right words, calls them 'dirty bastards'. If anyone's different from him, then he'll be prejudiced. If there's no reason, he'll invent one. Likes to be thought of as the last of a dying breed – a straight, working-class bloke. I think he's sick, sick, sick.

Mum started throwing up all over the place. Put the damper on her good-ish moods completely then. That, together with her craving for a fag. She looked better with a bit more weight, was eating like there was going to be a famine declared at any second. We'd eat together. Even if we weren't hungry, we'd eat. I hate the way Mum eats. Like a dog, makes noises.

Always either food to be eaten, or food to be bought. Bags and bags full. Tony gave her a lift back from the shops one morning, didn't think it was right that she should be carrying real heavy things in her condition. But someone saw and reported back to Bob in the pub. He was late home from work, it was past nine – his shift ended at half three. Mum was cross, our tea had been ruined – had to wait for him, he'd go up the wall if we had ours without him. When he finally came in he never even said sorry, or where he'd been or anything. Mum shouted at him.

'Bob, everything's bloody spoiled and . . . '

'Oh, listen to the lady of the house.'

He stank of whisky.

'Don't think of us, will you?'

'That sweet voice, that pretty face.'

'Stop being such a bloody child, Bob.'

He mocked, 'Oh, stop being such a bloody child, Bob, who do we think we are then?'

Mum put the red-hot plates on the table. We each took one, filled it with remnants of fried bacon, potatoes and sprouts. Always cooks that, thinks I really like it see. The gravy made it look worse. I sat and looked at it for a while, wondering whether to go without.

'Up to your usual standards I see.'

'Shut up, Bob. Eat it and shut up.'

'Well, actually, it's absolutely bloody disgusting, madam. What says the Queen? No? How about her Princess? Look at you both – like mother, like daughter.'

He laughed, not a real laugh.

'Know what they used to call your mother?'

'For Christ's sake, Bob.'

'Not ashamed surely? Thought you were proud of it. Stop off on the way home this morning? Good was it?'

He winked at me. I could've stabbed the bastard. Got up, left my tea, ran upstairs fast as I could. Shut the door, pushed the dressing table in front. Couldn't take it any more, couldn't.

Mum came up later on. Didn't let her in.

'He didn't mean to upset us, love, didn't mean anything . . . '

'It's not fair.'

'Life isn't about *fair*, it's about getting on with it, it's about making the best of a shit deal, it's about forgiving, forgetting.'

'But if you forget, how d'you ever expect to make things any better?'

'He's sorry to have upset you. He loves us. All three of us. Wasn't thinking, had too much to drink. Maybe loves us too much – gets jealous sometimes. People do get jealous when they really love someone, don't want to lose them. It won't happen again. Promise. And it was nothing really was it? A huge big fuss over nothing, all right? All right, love?'

So it was nothing. Sometimes, nothing is everything. If I could buy some explosives, paint them in glitter to disguise them, hide their sourness, then I'd hand them out to all these people, these horrid, horrid people who can't, won't, don't want to understand, know. I'd wait for each plastic person to growl, then howl, then bleed. That's what I'd do. I'd smile and say 'Bad luck – life's not about fair'.

But instead, what a minute and feeble speck on this earth I am. Once, Mum used to stroke my face, I'd look into her eyes, friendly eyes, always there for me if I felt sad. She didn't let me any more. You can't trust anyone. Not your mother, not anyone. Bob took my mum to bits. Took me to bits. Put us back together his way. Had us both. Like a wave, washing over us, smoothing away the identity. The salt is bitter. But Mum never learned how to run, and I'm afraid of the dark. Once I wished I could catch her voice, her touch, her scent – seal it in a jam jar with crunchy paper and an elastic band. Didn't want her lies any more. Had enough of my own.

Four

Quietness, go away, loudness, go away. The room that had been mine, but belonged to ghosts. I unstuck a cornflakes box, the one that'd been snarling as a dragon's head since I was little, used the plain inside to write on. Started off,

'I am not a virgin'

then,

'I let him do it'.

Ran my fingers over the sharp zig-zag teeth. Thought about what someone at school had said – that it's easy for a boy to tell if you're a virgin because girls always bleed the first time. Meant that one day, if I was to meet someone nice and marry him he'd know. And I wouldn't be good enough any more.

'Slut, tart, bitch'.

I tore the words into pieces, scattered them. They stared back. You can't just rip words up, they won't let you. Couldn't be read any more but still there, still able to touch. I was afraid that someone might find them, put them together like a jigsaw puzzle, so gathered them up again, tight in my fist. Made myself repeat what they said, a chant under my breath. Sweat made the bits stick to my palm, I went with them across the landing to the bathroom. Locked myself in, flushed them down the toilet. How pathetic crying becomes. But I still do it, all the time. About nothing. About telly, about someone speaking to me. The people and the noise, they tell you to hurry, to rush, but it's too fast, makes me sick and dizzy, I can't keep up.

Sophie had started saying that I'd got snappy and moody when there was no cause. Kept on about how lucky we are in this country and how we should learn respect. She loves to explain things like that. Loves to be seen to know. That's why she never minds helping people. She was for ever helping me, copied up homework, told me all the answers. Then she'd talk about when we would be sixteen or eighteen. How wonderful our lives would be. We'd go away, meets loads of new people, visit places that we never even knew existed. We'd live in a lovely place of our own and have parties that went on all week. The lucky ones. Interesting jobs, loads of money. We could buy clothes, especially black clothes – neither of our mums would let us wear black, said it made us look too old. Make-up. Lovely hair. Everything was going to be marvellous Sophie said, absolutely marvellous. We'd spend our dreams.

Her parents had just celebrated their twenty-fifth wedding anniversary. Twenty-five years is eternity I think. They had a dinner party – no kids invited. I told her that I'd be real upset if my mum had a do and said I couldn't go. She said I was too delicate. Said that I involve myself too much in things that don't concern me. By that she meant money and stuff – I'd told her about Mum not having enough, not being able to afford the things we needed. Sophie said that Mum'd manage because mums always manage, that's what they're good at. It's different for her, if you've got plenty of money like her family, then you don't have to worry, it doesn't matter, you just know you'll get by, and more. But if you haven't got any it's the difference between being warm and being cold, sleeping and lying awake. Money does matter, it matters a lot when there isn't any.

Sophie and me are different in loads of ways. There're lots of things that even a best friend is better off not knowing. Best friends are human too, in it for themselves, there's no point in selling yourself out. I could never talk to Sophie about really private things, like being so ugly. I was ashamed, still am, that I'm not nice for people to look at. I'm even ashamed of being ashamed. It'd embarrass her. Make her feel she had to say that it wasn't true, all the time I'd know that it was true. Kindness like that is a bit of an insult – I can see myself, I know.

When you're on your own you can be anything, anybody you choose. I can picture another me in my head. Not unlike the real one, but better, lively, popular, pretty. I can put a record on and be in another world – acting out scenes in my mind, with me in the leading, star-lit part. I'll never really be the other me, but it's a consolation prize to imagine. Almost a double life – one is sacred.

I did try to share the game with Sophie once, changed it a little, nothing to do with looks just tried to build a secret hide-out, a den, by dreaming. We were up in my room doing nothing, or relaxing as she puts it. Because it was something special for me, I thought it would be for her too. We could make another place, away from here, one where we could run at any time. I couldn't wait for all those years to pass before escaping.

'Close your eyes.'

'Why?'

'Go on. Close your eyes.'

'Closed.'

'Right. We are friends aren't we? Good friends?'

'Course. What is this?'

'A game.'

'What game?'

'I'll show you, I'll go first. We have to make a picture,

like a painting inside of ourselves.'

'Picture of what?'

I thought hard, it had to be perfect. Took time to get it right.

'Okay. A house. Old with diamondy windows. Daffodils, a cat, a dog, spiral stairs. An open fire and a coffee table with black glass on top. The carpets are white and the chairs velvet. I can play the piano, you prefer ballet. The lawns are greenest green and shortest short. But the woods are wild and exciting. We can switch the day on like a light, so the dark can never frighten us. Your turn. Your turn.'

She'd gone. Thought I was stupid.

Some of the time when no one else is around I spend ages playing games. Far from proud of it, too old to do that sort of thing now. So, I have to hide whatever it is I'm doing, pretend I'm not doing it. Make out I'm working or just being idle. I've painted the inside of the bike shed with water – used an old brush I found in the kitchen. Wrapped my hot water bottle in a pillow case, like a baby – it moved in the way I think a new born baby does move. I practised picking it up, rocking it gently, putting it down to sleep. I've done my nails by dipping a cotton bud in spit, loads of different things. Whenever I stop to think what it is I'm doing it infuriates me. I tell myself it's time I stopped playing, started being real, I punch the wall in temper and sometimes my knuckles are puffy and bruised, I have to keep my gloves on to hide the evidence on those days.

You can drown in your own weakness. It's less of a problem than struggling to swim, coping with the surge of tide. But it makes you feel so silly, like your bones would snap if somebody walked too close. You can hear laughter from people who think that because you don't talk much, you're rubbish, while they're funny and clever. I wish I could say to them, 'We'll see', because when the time comes, I'll use a sword, not a dumb mouth.

All the people and places started to make me feel ill. So ill that I couldn't tell the difference between ill and ordinary, it was all one, muddled together. Had to take a lot of time off school, could never say exactly why or what I was feeling. Mum made the diagnosis, 'runny tummy', 'migrane' or 'cold coming'. Always insisted that I stop away longer than was necessary, 'to be on the safe side'. Once, I was off for more than three weeks, lost touch a bit, school moves quickly.

Hadn't seen Sophie, or heard from her. It was unusual for her not to come buzzing round but Mum'd bumped into her and said that I was 'poorly and infectious', so I figured it was sensible she hadn't come. Sophie's always sensible and responsible. The last time I'd seen her though, we'd had an argument, good one, or bad one, depending how you look at it. She'd kept on at me all through assembly.

'Something to tell you. Important.'

She glowed at the thought, sung her heart out.

'*The Lord's my shepherd, I'll not want, He makes me down to lie, in pastures green, He leadeth me, the quiet waters by.*'

'You'll die of shock!'

Her whisper was loud and turned to a giggle, I couldn't bear the suspense of not knowing.

'*My soul He doth restore again, and me to walk doth make, within the paths of righteousness, even for His own name's sake.*'

'What? Tell me?'

'*Yea, though I walk in death's dark vale, yet will I fear none ill, for Thou art with me, and Thy rod, and staff me comfort still.*'

She hissed, 'You'll have to wait and see.'

'*My table Thou has furnished, in presence of my foes, my*

head Thou dost with oil anoint, and my cup overflows.'

'See you outside after.'

I'd never heard her sing with such power.

'*Goodness and mercy all my life, shall surely follow me, and in God's house for ever more, my dwelling place shall be.'*

Books shut, prayers said, chairs stacked.

'I saw *him.*'

'Who?'

'Well, hang on. Him – Bob.'

'So?'

'*Let me finish.* With a woman.'

'What woman?'

'How should I know – a woman, not your mum that's for sure.'

'And?'

'Well, it's obvious . . .'

'You didn't even see him.'

'Did.'

'Didn't.'

'Did.'

'Didn't.'

'Ask anyone, everybody knows, they're all talking.'

'Like who?'

'Like everyone.'

'Lies.'

'It's not lies.'

'Yes it is.'

'Oh grow up, thought you'd be glad.'

She stomped off. Liar. So damned pleased with herself. Thought I'd be glad! Bloody liar.

Then, the Saturday night before I went back, Bob sent me to the chippy to fetch some tea. Sophie was in the queue, at the front. I was pleased to see her again but tried to act ordinary because she hates it when people are overpowering, says that it suffocates her and she has to get away into her own space, whatever that means. I walked straight over but there was nothing wrong in that. Stood next to her.

'Hi.'

'Oh, it's you. Hi.'

She didn't ask me how I was but she did smile. Maybe she could see that I was better.

'What's been happening at school?'

'You've missed loads.'

'Don't care.'

'You should care.'

'What's the point?'

'A job, that's what.'

'Yeah, well. . .'

I wanted to say that I couldn't do it on my own, please help, show me. A stripy apron appeared with a little flat blob of a head on the top, balancing uncomfortably.

'Sausage and chips, doner kebab with chilli sauce.'

Sophie lifted the greasy parcels from the counter.

'We're going now. . .'

'Where?'

Another voice butted in.

'I was here before you, love.'

A big girl pushed me out of the way. I went to the end of the line. Sophie was grinning, so was *she*.

'See you Monday.'

So she'd found someone else to go around with. Melanie-seven-O-levels. Very actually actually fabulous. I hoped they'd both contract something terrible and die in the night. Suddenly I didn't count any more. I couldn't believe it, felt sad and envious. Course, she didn't actually say that I didn't count, but only because she didn't have the guts. I went round to sort it all out the next day, round to her place. *She* was there, sitting where I always sat. I just screamed through the living-room door,

'Fuck you.'

Her mum said I wasn't to go there again. Can't blame her. But it's like, we had always been friends, but now there was something that was too good for me to get near. Felt an idiot – shouldn't have been so soft. P'raps that's what she'd meant when she used to call me gullible and vulnerable. I felt wrecked, all she felt was sympathy and I hated that. Made me feel less. I looked forward to the day when sooper dooper smelly jelly dumped her – how pretty would she look then?

I scrawled things on the toilet walls at school:

'Sophie is a hor'

'Sophie likes gang bangs'

'Sophie's thing is like an apple core'

Told Mum about Melanie, she didn't get it.

'It's nothing is it? Don't be silly, love, find someone else, sod it.'

Reckon Sophie knew it was my graffiti. She never confronted me, doesn't like clashes. Ignored me, 'spect she decided it was the mature way of handling the situation, 'spect she told people that I couldn't be held responsible.

Unless I managed to gate-crash somebody else's group I was on my own. Funny how you can be surrounded by people and still be alone. New faces make me nervous, make me stutter and shake. I thought no one wanted me around, too dreary and miserable. The only thing I brightened up was the bus shelter.

'Melanie's got balls'

'Melanie does it with animals'

Went well alongside someone's 'Get it here – tel. 78787878' and 'It's not what you've got – it's how many you can give it to'. They'll wish they stayed friends when I'm a singer or an actress. Or a newsreader even.

Mum and Bob had begun to row nearly every day. I'd sit on top of the stairs at night, in my pyjamas, listening as they thrashed it out. They didn't know I was there. Mum was getting tired of waiting, Bob was fed up with her moaning. She sat around, drinking mugs of coffee, smoking, looking like a massive round ball of flab, terrible. Cried a lot. I did my best to help – with the house and that, but never seemed to feel like it. It was a tip. Just arguing and waiting, that's all there was. Everything was ready, except the baby.

They'd quarrel over anything, clothes not ironed, no soap, no toothpaste. One day Mum'd been short of maternity dresses and squeezed into an old pair of jeans, tight ones, couldn't do the zip up or anything but you could tell they were still uncomfortable. Bob came in, went crazy, it was 'his' baby again.

'Jesus Christ, woman, what the hell are you wearing? Want 'im to come out a spastic?'

Didn't give her time to answer, pushed her over – that's all the real concern he had – pulled the jeans off. She banged her head against the cooker, we both started to cry – I went off like a rocket.

'Bastard. Pig, pig.'

Mum got up, slapped my face.

'That's e-bloody-nough from you.'

Then she screamed at Bob.

'Where you bloody going now?'

He was storming off again.

'Nowhere, anywhere, God knows, away from you.'

She glared at me.

'Now see what you've done, get out of my way, go to bed.'

'You deserve Bob, Mum, you deserve everything you get.'

Right then I meant it.

I didn't go to bed, didn't go anywhere. He'd done it again, made us fight, it wasn't our battle.

We sat there in silence, like a game, the first one to

give in would be the loser. Really we were both losers. Mum kept folding her arms then unfolding them, pretending to be fine, pretending to be taken up with every inch of the room, except the portion that contained me. I sat in Dad's chair, picked at the fabric tape that'd mended a slit in the seat. It was sticky and curled up at the ends, the colour didn't match exactly, it was horrid. Mum was wanting to tell me off, tell me to stop it but she didn't, acted like she wasn't concerned, looked like a wild woman though. When Bob got back home, me and her would be all right again. He always marked the beginning and the end of everything.

Except he didn't come home like he usually did after a slanging match. We both watched the clock, waiting for him, like waiting for God to appear or something. Got later and later.

I looked at Mum, trying to make my face ask her to speak to me. Her expression gradually changed. Her voice was all high-pitched and squeaky, not her voice at all.

'Where the hell is he? What's happened to him?

I moved my chair next to hers, side by side.

'What if he's had an accident? Or's in trouble?'

She started talking rubbish. Made excuses for him, why he hadn't been in touch, where he was. Went on about how she'd neglected him lately but was going to make a real effort in the future. Everything was going to be perfect. He'd be such a proud father, he'd stop in with us all the time, we'd be a proper family. She was always saying that, proper family. We sat up till gone seven in the morning.

As he walked in, I saw her face search his for news of some terrible happening. He went straight by, smiling.

'Lovely morning for it. . .'

The wood of the stairs creaked with his weight.

'I should've been a better wife to him. Treated him better.'

'He's a bastard, Mum, *he is*. He's a pig.'

But she was staring away from me, don't know if she even heard.

'It's my fault. I should've been a better wife.'

I yelled at her.

'Shut up! Don't say that, I can't stand it.'

She didn't stir.

'You'll understand, one day, when you're older.'

Inside I burst. Kicked the sideboard, it was that, or her. She went upstairs to him, I went out, walked. God, she was so afraid. Of losing him, of being on her own. I couldn't feel sympathy.

I don't like Dad and Vicky's place, only go there when there's nowhere else. Dad had only just found out that Mum was expecting. Or so he said. He was mad at me for not letting on earlier – didn't matter that I hadn't seen him for months, he still wanted to be kept up to date on her every movement. It wasn't on purpose – I thought he'd be bound to know already and didn't see the point in mentioning it, I knew what it'd be like. He more or less accused me of lying to him.

'That's great. I thought you would have told me at least. That's very bloody nice, everybody knows, except me.'

'I thought you did know.'

'Oh, you did, did you? Look, if your mother wants to start up trouble by turning you against me. . .'

'It's nothing to do with Mum. I thought you knew, that's all.'

'You can tell me, I am your father. She told you not to say anything?'

'No. I said.'

'Just up her street. Always been the same. Never change a woman like her.'

Why today? Today of all days?

'Still, we'll see what happens when this baby comes.

Shut you out that's for sure. P'raps then *you'll* see it too.'

I'd never lied to Dad. Couldn't see why it meant so much to him, but I'd never lied.

Vicky hasn't got time for me. Don't s'pose I can expect her to, to her Mum's the 'other woman', I'm the 'other woman's' child. It's like when I go to their house, I take a bit of Mum with me. She's bound to crop up in the conversation, the only thing me and Dad have in common. Mum calls Vicky 'the slag'.

After Dad left us, he'd sneak back some afternoons, him and Mum would disppear, spend a few hours together. It was torture for her, all the time she thought he might come back for keeps she couldn't begin to forget him while there was still that chance. They've always fought over me. Only because neither wants the other to win, nothing to do with me, the person. Whenever I fall out with Mum she says 'You're like your father'. When I fall out with Dad he threatens to boycott my wedding. If I do get married, I don't think I'd have either of them there, however much I wanted them to come. They'd try and upstage each other, end up spoiling things. And it wouldn't be fair to choose between the two and only invite one.

I think they love each other and hate each other at the same time. The way they look at one another frightens me, like they're about to attack, though I'm never quite sure why. Dad was jealous of the baby, I could tell. Didn't like to think that another man had taken his place in her life, even though he didn't want her for himself. He was bitter over Bob, almost as if he'd expected Mum to sit at home and wait for him in case he ever decided he needed her for something.

Dad's still good-looking even though he's going grey. It's a nice grey. Always smart, a bit flashy. Vicky dresses up a lot too. Some people seem to be able to wear anything and look nice. Mum questions me about her – have I seen her? What did she say? What was she wearing? Did it look new? What about her hairstyle? Mum's pretty scared that I might actually get to like Vicky, she doesn't want that. It's all right to chat, but she can't bear to think that she might figure in my life in any bigger way. She needn't worry, more like a sister that I don't get along with too well, or not even that. Only in her twenties, not much older than me really. Well, a lot younger than Mum, so she'd better not try to push me around.

I didn't want to go back home that afternoon, there wasn't much option after drifting round for half the day. Stopped off at the phone box in the end of our road, dialled 999. I'd never done it before, it was easy. They asked me my name, I had to make one up quick but it helped to give the impression of total panic. Called the fire brigade for Sophie's house.

Mum was hidden among cans of paint and rolls of paper. She'd decided to redecorate the front room before the baby came, instead of after. Had the long table out, mixed up the paste, found the big scissors. She didn't bother to strip the old stuff off, just carried on over the top. I must have watched her for an hour or more before she said anything. She was working real fast, as if she was throwing herself into the job completely, but I knew she wasn't.

'All right, love? Gunna look nice.'

'Where's Bob?'

'Work course.'

'You shouldn't be doing all this. He should help you.'

She forced a laugh.

'Can't if he's at work can he?'

Her eyes were red, she was biting her bottom lip.

'Been to see Dad.'

She didn't answer, but reacted by slapping the glue on

to the paper even more viciously than before. When she picked up that particular piece it stuck to itself and was ruined.

'He said he didn't know you were pregnant. Was angry with me and. . .'

'Not now, love, eh . . .'

She screwed up the spoiled bit, twisted it round like she was wringing someone's neck. Then she sighed real heavily, looked round at me and smiled.

'How long d'you reckon it'll take?'

'Be quicker if *he* was helping you.'

'Be quicker if *you* were helping me.'

'Well I'm not. It's not my house.'

I'd planned to say that, rehearsed the next bit too, waited for the right slot to fill. She was shocked.

'What d'you mean by that? Course it's your house, you live here don't you?'

'All right then, it is my house, but it's not my home and never will be again.'

It'd come out just like I'd wanted, I was pleased. Mum turned dead nasty, I wanted that too, wanted to hurt her for being so stupid.

'And where is your home then?'

'With Dad.'

She sort of leapt across the room, looking like the devil. Caught hold of me by the shoulders, pressing really hard with her nails.

'Now you bloody listen to me . . .'

But she couldn't say it, she crumpled up in the chair, put her hands over her face and cried out loud. Her eyeliner smudged and made railway tracks on her skin, blotches of black goo.

'I've done my best. Can't do any more. Can't do more than that.'

I didn't feel sorry, I felt like hitting her some more only with my feet and hands instead of my tongue.

'*You* brought him here Mum.'

To watch her pain felt good. She put her hair straight, wiped her face over.

'And I'll keep him here, God knows, somehow I'll keep him.'

I'd like to hide behind the wallpaper, jump out at people unexpectedly. To make up for all those times they've made me feel stupid and confused. My shape would be torn away, the dust would outline my body and look like magic and spook. Then I'd jump back in, the ripped paper would repair and reseal itself leaving them all bewildered. No one would like to say anything in case they'd hallucinated and were thought insane. I'd be peeping out through a seam, laughing to myself.

At school absolutely everyone had heard about Sophie's fire engine. It made me feel incredibly important to think I'd caused an event of such interest. And to think that I knew something that the others didn't know, but desperately wanted to know. When I listened to all the talk it made my heart thud – felt like I was going on holiday or out to spend loads of money. I liked that feeling a lot. Bad's better than good.

I had to see the Head of our year – nothing connected with the emergency call – 'they' had come to think that I may be better suited to a lower grouping. Wanted to hear what I had to say before taking any steps. Face like a half-done jacket potato, her office more like a cell. She sipped black coffee from a china cup, smoked king-sized cigarettes, brown ones not white, all thin and smelly. There were five telephones on her desk.

She asked me if anything had upset me recently. If there was any reason I could think of, as to why my work had deteriorated. Said about problems with other girls, had I found the work increasingly difficult or was it a sudden thing rather than gradual. Asked if I thought

I'd be happier with the pace slowed down a bit. Bullshit. I gave the answers she wanted to hear, it wasn't difficult. Actually pretending to be interested in me. What odds is it to her what I might do when I leave school? Yes, I had set my heart on something actually, now you come to mention it.

I smirked at her.

'I'd like to be an astronaut.'

Her eyes went small. It was thereon decided that I'd be 'more comfortable' in a lower set, one where I was better suited, etc. Said I'd been misplaced at the beginning of the year.

'You see, even we teachers make mistakes sometimes – and you thought we were perfect!'

That was meant to be funny but she looked at me as if to say, 'Another word from you and you're dead . . . '

I pulled on the door handle without looking back, eager to get out, went straight to the toilet, like a hole in the ground to a rabbit.

'God is a spaceman'

'The world wanks'

Then I made up a story. Made things happen to other people as well, not just me.

Once upon a time there was a girl. She was ordinary. She had a sister. An average sister. Their father, he made love to the elder – she was his fantasy within reality. They were devoted to the point of obsession. But the second daughter, she was different. It's not easy to come to terms with being different. Why didn't she see him as something special too? The first person, the beginning, the root, *is* special, or should be. One degraded the other, it gave him erections, so he got drunk and raped her. He can't remember much about it now. But he never forgets to pick flowers from the garden, place them on her grave each morning, as he winds his way to the daily slog of an office routine. Even though he gets a parking ticket on the Jag several times per month. Company pays.

The kids in the next group down had their own problems. From the first day, I didn't even consider joining in, just a joke. I sit right at the back if I can, hide behind a boy called Graeme. His shirts are too tight and his body underneath looks like it's trying to get out. I hate hairy hands. Graeme's sprouting them already, and most of the men teachers have them. The one I hate most wore sandals all through winter, his mane hangs, limp and greasy. He never calls anyone by their christian name, always their surname or just 'girl', or 'boy'. Shouted at me once for 'carrying the distinct odour of tobacco'. Spit shot out of his mouth as he launched into how many people die through things that are no fault of their own, here was a silly little girl smothering her lungs, killing herself slowly, out of choice. Showed me up in front of everyone, waving those gorilla hands about. Couldn't wait for breaktime so's I could have a fag to help me over it, skived his next session.

I hate breaktime, I hate dinnertime. Being on your own makes the sun cold, the cold colder. It's like everyone's looking at me, horrible, standing around on your own, people wondering why you've got no friends, must be something wrong with you. We're only allowed inside if it's throwing down buckets of rain, or to go to the loo. The older kids on door duty always seem to remember if you've already been and won't let you back in to go again, don't believe that you could need to wee a second time. And it gets so cold outside.

I never told Mum about changing groups. She'd tell me off and ask loads about *why* it'd happened. She might even get in touch with the school, probably start accusing them of something. Not that it'd really bother her, or that she'd understand it very well, just likes something to get her teeth into. Trying.

Bob's spell of employment was brief. A combination of being idle, being late and not turning up at all. He just laughed it off, came out with 'their loss' and equally ridiculous statements. Said they didn't know how to run a business, found him threatening to their authority because he'd twigged on to solving problems that had mystified them for years. Wasn't going to drink in there again, fill 'their' pockets, they didn't deserve good custom. Mum was worried, anyone could see that. She didn't say much to him, not sure if she agreed so's to keep the peace or if she really did believe what he'd said. There was only his dole money from then on. He said 'everybody's on the dole' as if that made it all right. I even went there with him and Mum once, to see if we could get more money. He reckoned it'd look better if the whole family turned up looking depressed and desperate. I'm not sure which, but it should either be compulsory that kids go there and see – to make them fight to save themselves – or they should never be subjected to such shit. I wanted to scream and shout before we all melted together. Out of control people, lumps of wasted meat. Each one looked the same, I merged so well. Nobody was happy, nobody was kind, everybody was a nobody. AND SO MANY OF THEM. Brains go clank, clank, eyes gradually fill. My God, they're angry. They might shuffle and look dead but it's the anger that makes them shiver, not the cold stone, chill as it is.

The rest of the world disown you, like you stink. Like you're fading out of yourself and into someone horrid who you don't like and don't want to be. And I wish people'd stop talking about going 'away' to find work, to make it all better. Where is this place 'away'? I wish we were all just people, instead of there being grey people and red people. It's like everyone gets a draw ticket, only sometimes the winning portion of your ticket gets thrown away before the draw – unless you're deepest scarlet. I read this thing once, a religious message – advert in the paper – said that most of the world's problems are caused by man's greed. They're wrong. You've *got* to be greedy, if you lose your hunger, then you really are the living dead.

Mum'd finished her job of course. I'm not sure if she was getting any sort of allowance or grant, but I know there wasn't enough money to get by on. She started eyeing up bits and pieces around the house, wondering how much they'd sell for at the car-boot sale. In the end she found out a whole load of stuff that we could do without. Her sewing machine, bedside table, lamp, few clothes, old shoes, a wooden paper rack, metal jewellery, beads, a handbag, umbrella, camera (the one with the film in), an iron that didn't work, talcum powder and soap set, ornaments, old records, painting by numbers, bike pump. Took it to the ground where the market was held on the next Saturday. The car was bursting. Priced everything roughly, but over the top, so's she could knock a bit off to make the buyers think they were getting a better deal, like real market people do. It wasn't easy, knowing what to ask but I think she marked most of the stuff pretty fairly.

Turned out that everything sold except one pair of shoes. Made her wonder if she'd been too generous, too late to worry though. The entrance fee was a fiver. Deducted from the takings it left Mum with twenty-six fifty.

Gran thought it was disgusting, selling from your own home but I noticed she didn't come forward with any offer of financial support. I told Mum that I was proud of her for what she'd done and I was, can't be easy to dismantle your belongings, even if they weren't much use. Like stepping down and saying, 'I'm so poor that I have to bargain my own things for as much as I can get'. She answered that the possibility was there, so, she took advantage of it. Said that chances don't just happen, you have to make them happen. And make them work. Said that what other people think of you isn't important, ridicule is nothing to be afraid of.

I wish I could have helped God invent the world. I wouldn't have made dirt dirty. It'd be soft like snow but not cold. Then I wouldn't mind the dirt inside of me so much. Things that are terrible could be undone, unpicked like knitting. There'd be less shouting, more singing. Winter would be summer, summer would be Paradise. And roads would be made of silver and rubies. There'd be no such thing as a hunter. Though when a hound's on the scent of a fox, when the chase is done and the dog's tracked it down, then at least it rips the victim's throat out, bleeds it to death. At least a cat, after it's tortured a mouse, tossed it from paw to paw, scraped it along the gravel, up into the air, goes on to eat the squealing creature. Spiders and flies, birds and worms. Yet we think they're below us, that we're so clever. They might not care too much about the pain they inflict but they do end it. And it doesn't take them months or years. Like ten, twenty, thirty *years*. I'd be an animal all right, if I could. One that could get even by being feared. Touch people's defences.

All those years to come. Coffee? Tea? Vodka? Pull yourself together, can't really be that bad. Forget about it, get on with your life, put it behind you, what's past is gone. It was yonks ago. Think of the future, your future, you're still young. Things look good, make the best of them, you'll be fine. You're all right, *really*. Stop making excuses for yourself.

Why not try some highlights? Or lowlights? Buy something nice, parfum – sophisticated, sexy, young, carefree. Something tight, shiny, velvet to the touch. Black dress, gold jewellery, elegant, attractive. Shades for the season, they'll make you glow, on fire, with passion, with lust,, with contentment. Well, if you won't help yourself . . .

Five

Bob was snatching things up off the bedroom floor, shirts, trousers, socks. Stuffed each crumpled old rag into one of about ten carriers, heaped on the bed, splitting at the seams.

'*Please*, Bob, don't. Please don't.'

Jumpers, alarm clock, razor, training shoes. One of the bags tipped over and emptied, he sunk his fist into it and started again.

Oh don't cry, Mum. Hate it when you cry.

'I'll do anything at all, change. Be whoever you want me to be.'

'Too fucking late.'

'What about *us*, *our* marriage, *our* baby? Bob. . . '

'You'll think of something.'

'We've built so much together, can't just throw it all away.'

'As far as I can see there's nothing to throw away. Nothing.'

'Bob. I *love* you.'

'Look, I don't need this.'

I'll take care of you, Mum, I will.

'Our child needs you, needs a father. I need you. Want you.'

More socks, T-shirts, boots.

'Bob, I'll die without you. *I'll die.*'

I love you, Mum.

'You'll be all right.'

'No. Where're you going?'

'Doesn't matter.'

'You can't just go, Bob, you can't.'

'*I don't need this crap*, now get out of my way.'

'Bob, look at me. Can you tell me, honestly, that you don't love me?'

'I don't.'

Her scream made me prick with hurt.

Walk in, walk out. What a waste of time. What a waste of Mum, of a baby. No challenge for him any more. She let him trample on her until he'd had all there was to have. Walked away, just like a stranger.

She cut the meringuey dress into shreds, set a light to them in the garden. Bashed her ring flat with a hammer. She'd got both their rings, from the catalogue. Bob only wore his the once, never saw it again. Gran said it would've been better if she'd sold the stuff not ruined it, but Mum didn't care about her, what she thought didn't matter any more. Kept going through Baby M's things, the clothes especially. Touching, looking, then she'd hold her bump, tell it how much she loved it, how everything was going to work out in the end.

Kept saying about no one giving a shit for anyone else. I wish she'd be different but the same, in ways. Wish she wouldn't give so much of herself over to people. Wish she'd save some back for the rough times. And that she'd learn instead of standing still. She said that all men are bastards – but she's not entitled to say that, nobody is. If someone is foolish enough to allow it, then that person will always find a bastard to oblige. We should have shut him out, right from the start. If only she had had more pride and I more nerve.

I go down to the railway station sometimes. To look. Try to figure things out. I see a hundred faces like my mum's. Growing older and impatient, scared of collecting dust. I wonder who thought it his or her job to make being constantly scared into a slum feeling for second-class people. So scared of being scared. . .

Gappy-toothed bank workers in wedge-heeled sandals, crimpeline skirts and pastel cardigans, red-haired and freckle-faced. Ten years ago girls, nylony bloused, suede shoulder-bagged with tits pushed up to their chins. Punks and bosses inhaling the same air, being fed the same rubbish, though neither would admit it.

The platforms are tarmac and match the commuters. Only one strip is wooden, that's the piece I always go to. Just five planks of grubby brownness. Crouching down, rubbing my fingers across it makes me feel shivery. So does the scrambling, the urgency.

'Get a move on. . . '

'Come on. Come on, we're late. . . '

'Always the same. . . '

'This is the very last time. . . '

'Hurry up. . . '

'If *we* miss this one. . . '

And off they go. Never slowing down to take stock, must keep up, must keep up. At that moment no one could move me. I *won't* do what I don't want to, what I don't like.

I love the power of the trains, no feeling, no hurt. Giant, mile-long caterpillars. They're in control. They whiz by at a thousand miles per hour because it's fun for them. Because they want to make everything, everyone, bow down to them. Any creature, any flower, they'll crush, determined and strong. I have to tell myself – choice, there must be a choice, the giver or the taker.

Over, over again. Cases and bags. Crying and not much kissing.

I've not travelled by train. If I ever do I shan't behave

like the other passengers. Won't buy a ticket, get a seat, that's for sure. I'll just jump on, cling to the outside, at the back I think would be best. A gentle breeze, then a gust, then a whirling tornado. Floating my body out straight, a satiny ribbon in the wind. The caramel sun would watch as I passed through the towns and valleys. Kicking out I'd strike the dirty factory chimneys, the plasticy offices, the milky-white shops. Smash them to the ground, tumbling like a stack of playing cards, into rubble marked by my trail. People, all people, would remember that day, tell their children and their grand-children, about the day when I came by.

No one knows about me. Not anything about me. I'm glad because it means that I'm able to wake them up whenever I want. The shock of the unexpected. When I'm older, that's just what I'll do, I'll show them, let them know who I am. They'll be sorry for messing with me. I'll make them *want* to take notice. When I'm older, when I've left school, you wait and see.

It's funny, school. When they realise that you're not going to excel, not going to give them cause for great pride and credit they don't bother with you. It's them who do the deciding. Instead of trying to get the best from you they just conclude that you've slotted into the place where you belong. That's a more convenient method.

The fire brigade incident was mentioned loads of times in assembly, the culprit asked to own up if he or she was present. Sophie's parents had apparently been insistent that it must have been someone from the school, demanded that everything possible be done to find out more. While all this was going on, the gathering of information and that, I s'pose Sophie was remaining 'adult' by not grassing. I loved that special feeling. At the earliest opportunity I dismantled the tampon dispenser, shoved it down one of the pans.

Didn't even bother to take the boxes out. The fuss gave me something to look forward to, little me, if only they knew. Catch me if you can, the guessing game. Disruption really matters to some people, really gets to them. Ha bloody ha.

It was a few days before Bob came round. I was on my own but pretended that Gran was upstairs, was determined not to let him in.

'Want some stuff.'

'Come back when Mum's here.'

'Where is she?'

'Shopping.'

'Out with a new bloke?'

'No.'

'Won't take her long to find one.'

'Just piss off, Bob, come back when Mum's here.'

'You're not stopping me from coming in my own bloody house if you think you are.'

'Not your house.'

'Listen, I'm your mother's husband, right? That makes it my house.'

'She'll be back soon.'

He pushed me out of the way.

'When I married her, when I bought the licence, I bought rights, legal rights. It's all down on paper – house and all. Rights to be in control, to the things we've got, to fuck her if, and when, I feel like it. And she's not taking all my gear when you go.'

'Go where?'

'Leave, move out little girl, hasn't she told you?'

'I'll tell her what you did to me at Christmas.'

'Bollocks you will, who d'you think's gunna believe your pathetic little tale?'

I ran down the path, fast as I could. Along the street, towards the shops. Couldn't find Mum anywhere. Eventually I gave up.

I was late home, the door had been left open, it'd rained hard, soaked the floor. She was fuming.

'Where've you been?'

'Bob came round, I went out, to look for you.'

'I can bloody see that Bob came round. Taken a load of stuff.'

'I told him to wait till you got back.'

'Your radio's gone. Your own fault, shouldn't have bloody let him in.'

'Couldn't stop him.'

'Silly bloody fool.'

'It's not my fault.'

'All the bloody doors left open.'

'He said that we're going somewhere else, to live.'

'He bloody would. Look. Don't you think I've got enough on my plate? Can't you try to see what I'm going through?'

She cried. Again. I wondered if she cried just to get out of things, make me feel guilty.

'But is it true?'

'Oh Christ, not now. Lay off. Just lay off.'

Later I asked her if it was my fault. She said no, whispered that when she thinks of me the hurt isn't so bad. Where are you, Mum? Are you in my world? Am I in yours? I can see you but I can't get close. One of us in a steel cage, the other in a broken glass case. Can't we be the train, mow it all down? But then I s'pose we'd lose the daisies and the buttercups too.

Bob got our house. Don't know why or how. Don't care, he had it, the end. We moved into a flat just before Mikey was due to be born. A flat with dirty windows, high up in the sky. Adolf had to stay behind, but apart from that we made it as comfy as we could with all our old things.

Dad came to see us but Mum wouldn't let him in. She never has anyone in, or goes out. It's a bit difficult to find someone reliable to mind the baby. I've offered but she knows I'd be a bit worried if she took me up on it – don't have much experience, see. Gran's too far away and we don't really know many people, not anyone who'd be suitable, who Mum'd trust enough. We sit and watch telly, like always, only more.

Mikey sleeps in Mum's room, though he doesn't seem to sleep much at all. Not at night anyway. I don't mind, got used to it, but Mum's sometimes so tired that she just sits down and wails with him. He's a lovely little boy, all pink with dark hair and brown eyes. His toes and fingers curl up when I poke them and he's got one of those funny sticky-out belly buttons. Mine goes inwards, all folded away neatly. At times the look on his face is so funny that we laugh until our bellies ache.

Reckon we're here for good. Takes some getting used to – everything on one level, seems like we're sleeping downstairs except you know that you're up in the sky, the clouds all around. It's ever so different, stepping outside the front door, not into air, but into a dim corridor. There's no writing or dirt, just cold and hard. We can hear what the people above, below and to the sides are saying to each other. I s'pose they hear us too. Surrounded by real people, breathing, yet you never ever actually see them. I swear that when the wind blows we rock, sway over the trees. If there were any. Maybe if one day we fall over, then we'll get to meet the people who live here with us.

I wonder who chose the colours, yellow and grey. I'd like to find out if we're allowed to change them but the planners don't live anywhere near.

Mum's got a poster of Clint Eastwood in the broom cupboard. He jumps out as the door's opened – always tell when she's about to start the cleaning.

'Oh, Clint, not now.'

Says that for a laugh. She's real tubby again, since the

baby. Her tum bounces and I feel like I want to tap it with a stick, watch to see if it wobbles. I wonder whether it's hard or soft, soft I think, like a slice of tripe, squidgy blubber. I spotted her naked the other day, the tops of her legs are all dimply, fat and thin at the same time, nothing's even, either too big or too small. Not like the girls in our newspaper. When Mum bends down to wipe the lino her bum pushes right out and her legs take on a whole new shape, like they're only borrowed.

She never speaks like other people speak. Used to, but now she shouts, hollers, no matter if she's mad or happy, upset or just nothing. I think the rest of the world is frightened of my mum and me, the same as we're frightened of them.

Sometimes, when I have daydreams of being rich and famous, I wonder what I'd feel about her if it really did happen. I wonder if I'd fly away and leave her, or if I'd give and share. I wonder if – then – she'd be my friend.

Vicky's expecting. They're not married. Not intending to get married either. Vicky says there's more respect that way – if the other person has no hold on you. Makes people try harder, work at making things good. She says that she doesn't need a public declaration to make her feel secure – their private promises mean more, telling the whole world would only cheapen the situation. Reckons on going back to work once her baby's arrived and is on the right road. A job gives her some independence and she likes her own money to spend how she pleases, waste it if she feels like it. Says the benefit of remaining single is that you can be irresponsible and have no one to answer to but yourself. I don't think she ever is irresponsible, not really, just likes to know that she can be if she wants. Independence, choice, right – she uses those words a lot. It's bound to alter things, a baby, but she won't change herself – everything around will have to adapt the best it can. Vicky copes, always determined to battle on against defeat. Mum says she's a hard cow.

Don't know why people go in for kids sometimes. Mum had Mikey because Bob thought he wanted him, then decided he didn't after all. Vicky wanted one, I'll bet, because Dad and Mum had me and she didn't want to be less important than Mum. Perhaps she is irresponsible. Mum and Dad had me because it was an accident. It's weird to think that you weren't meant to be here. S'pect they cried when they found out I was coming. S'pect they would have done anything to turn the clock back, not have me. Though Mum did say once that giving birth was the most painful thing, but the most wonderful thing. Painful physically, like a terrible rolling in your stomach, but the best day of her life.

I couldn't stand it the day Dad had left us. It was like, final. I kept on asking him, why? He'd never answer. I thought it was the least he could do, explain, tell me about it. But he didn't, wouldn't. I thought of the times we'd gone out together, the times he'd told me off. And the nice things he'd said, about being special, a special girl, it was all rubbish. When I was small he called me Cathy. I loved that. He'd stand up for me when Mum got cross, say I hadn't done anything wrong when he knew that I had. Sometimes he encouraged me to be a bit naughty, it was fun. Mum didn't think so, she was always too busy to join in anyway. I can't ever remember if he read to me, but we'd play snap. I used to get fed up – he always let me win, thinking I didn't know that he'd meant to lose. Made it dead boring. We used to go on day trips too. Every Sunday through the summer. It was like being in heaven.

This year summer was an absolute wash-out, rain, rain, rain. Had to stay inside most of the time. Not much room, that was the trouble, I was always in the way. And I got roped in to helping. Not the weather for pram pushing that's for certain, pity, I'd looked forward to it. But at least it meant that we didn't need to get the pram wheel fixed. I tried to mend it but it needed an expert, made it worse Mum said. It's not wasted though, the top can be lifted away from the frame, used as a carry cot. The blue crinkly material isn't very good, shows every stain, can't be wiped clean.

Mum's said all along that she'd definitely be having Mikey christened, now the time's come she's changed her mind. I don't see the point, she doesn't believe in God. Don't know if that's why she's decided against it, shouldn't have thought so, it's never stopped her taking part in churchy events before. Would've gotten married in church if they'd let her. Not right that. Using somebody else's place, somewhere that's real important to them, just because it's more attractive, prettier than any of the alternatives. Quite an insult to 'believers'. Not that going to church and saying you believe makes you good. Mum doesn't think of church and religion as being related, but nothing to do with the fact that you can be a Christian without having to show everyone, just that the building is there and she won't let any 'snob' stop her from going to it, using it, if that's what she wants to do. We tried the christening robe on Mikey, the same one that Mum, and then I, had worn. Didn't fit, he was a big baby. S'pect she made her mind up then, had nothing suitable to dress him in. She'd wanted him done, I think, because everyone else has their kids done. But wouldn't be shown up by lack of frilly posh clothes.

I do like my brother, though the novelty wears off. Takes so much time to care for a baby, I didn't realise, they're so *completely* helpless. Cost a lot too. If Mum heard me talk like that she'd go up the wall. She's trying to get Bob to come back to her. Can't say what I think, don't know. I know that Mikey deserves a father, but does he need one just for the sake of it? Bob comes round all the time. It's the same as it was, except two separate houses. They go to bed though Mum says they don't. The other day, when there was a bomb on telly, on the news, Mum said, 'God. Fuck me . . . '

Bob said, 'What, again? I just did . . . '

The train burrs, no feeling, no hurt, no feeling, no hurt. The carriages link, but never pour as one, if they did, they'd crash. Torn hot metal maims and disfigures. Got to balance yourself, not too hard, not too soft. The station gets full to the brim, overflowing with ladies in furs, tight black trousers and pink boots. Go on, fling yourself at the driver.

'Taxi.'

The dead rabbits on her back moult, make him sniffle. And angry. Doesn't want to do the job. But what else can he do? Say that he's already booked, go home, that's what. The train twists for no one. Got to do what's right for you.

Litter, litter everywhere. Except on the track. 'Real ice-cream lollipop', 'Real milk chocolate', 'Real home-made pie'. Please God, blow *me* away too. Let *me* glide to another place.

An old lady, pock-filled face, waiting to catch the five fifty. It's always late. Exactly five minutes late. Don't know why they don't call it the five fifty-five instead. Wealthy, easy to see. Rich in 'things'. No one to talk to. No one to cuddle. A woollen suit, bet the label said 'pure' and 'new'. A felt hat – couldn't see a gold pin but there probably was one. No fags or booze in that leather handbag, not even for emergencies. Why doesn't someone cosh her over the head? Watch her support tights fall down to the ground? Watch that grace turn to ordinary, turn into the rest of us? Bet she had lovers *then*, but not *now*. A tall blond soldier. *Sipping* sherry. Yes, the prettiest girl he'd ever seen, when he could stop laughing. She wouldn't see his smirk, just blush and look away with pride. As he was leaving he'd say, 'I shall miss you . . .'

Then he'd touch her and she'd gasp in amazement.

'No!'

'Don't you love me? Love me like I love you?'

'Yes, but. . .'

He'd raise his forefinger to his lip.

'Shhh. It's all right. . .'

Ten minutes later he'd be gone. She'd never see him again.

Dad sent Mum a bottle of gin, her favourite. Well, he didn't actually send it, he gave it to me to pass on. She's usually knackered all the time, irritable, but was really pleased with the drink, knocked it back.

I like to find out about her. Her secrets. Like to know if she's ever felt like I feel. I've asked her loads, about when she was young. Younger. She starts off by saying that it wasn't 'too' long ago, that she was, well, a bit older than me. And of course, she had far less than I've got, but appreciated it more. Times weren't so cushy then, much stricter, not the opportunities of today. She says that I make her feel old. I love it when she tells me about the things she's got up to, things that Gran still doesn't know anything about. I've heard it all a million times before but it never loses anything for telling. Memories make Mum smile. I asked her what her very first boyfriend was like – she's always hinting to me about boys I know. She didn't have to think too hard.

'Fat.'

'Is that all, fat?'

'Fat, spotty, but quite nice. I s'pose. Nice personality.'

'What was his name?'

'Clive. I hate that name, worse than Dennis.'

Dennis is Dad's name, Den for short.

'How old were you?'

' 'Bout your age, bit younger even.'

'And how long did you go out?'

'Three days, didn't really "go out", just, well, I don't know, I was his girlfriend, he was my boyfriend.'

'How many boyfriends did you have before Dad then?'

She laughed, not really minding.

'What is this, the bloody SS? Oh, God knows, too many, if there is such a thing. Clive was first, then, no, then . . . '

She juggled with them, I didn't give her much chance to sort them out.

'Where did you meet Dad?'

'Dance. Fancied him for ages, weeks before we actually spoke, both of us shy.'

'What made you like him?'

'Looks, motorbike, leathers.'

'Did you? You know, a lot. Before you were married – or just once?'

'Cheeky sod! What a question to ask your bloody mother! Couple of times, now and again. Course we did.'

'What, quite often? How often?'

'Don't sound so shocked! And don't be so naive as I was. Wasn't very nice going home to Gran, telling her I was pregnant. In fact it was bloody terrible. Thought our dad'd kill your father – chased him out of the house, right up the street. The neighbours loved it, they soon guessed what it was all about.'

'What made you do IT?'

'Well . . . '

'What?'

'Well. When you meet someone you like. It just happened. You'll be on the Pill but it happened to me like it happened to my mother, and her mother before her.'

'Gran!'

'Yes, love, Gran.'

It stunned me into a silence for a while. Gran!

'Has anyone ever asked you to, to, do IT, when you didn't want to?'

'No – I always wanted to!'

She noticed my expression straight off.

'Oh, all right, baby, it's a joke, bit of fun. You know, ha ha. That's the trouble with you, don't have a laugh, see the funny side. Don't be so serious all the time, can't get through life like that.'

But I didn't think it was funny. Just wanted to know if she knew what it felt like. If I thought she did, *someone* did, then I'd feel a whole lot better, I think. She had no idea though.

It doesn't go away because it's a separate thing, not mine to take charge of. I stick my fingers between my legs and make myself remember what I let him do. I push them inside until it hurts so much. Then I'm there again, can feel the hard ground, the wetness, smell the beer and the breath. But I just can't fight. If only I could fight then it'd all be mended. I can't and the hurt turns to a tingle. I like it. I want someone to just know. Not say, but know. I can't say it. It'd be easier to die.

I mustn't ever tell, admit it. And if I had? I'm so glad I didn't. Is she telling the truth? Has she made it all up? Jealousy, attention? Could ruin an innocent man. Let's go to court, let the jury decide. Let her repeat the tale again, to a room packed full with strangers. See if we can trick her, find the truth. See if she can still remember what she accused him of, all those months ago. Of course, if he is guilty, he'll get what he deserves. Couple of years? And the way things are looking she might be able to claim, you know, compensation, cash. Yes, let's take a chance, rip her to shreds then force her to watch the action replay. And don't worry, if it gets too ugly – look the other way.

I wish Adolf was here. Made Mum laugh, the way I was with him. Said I was a bloody nutter. He understood. More than her. Once, when I was about six or seven, Dad bought me a walky-talky doll. A present from a skittles outing to somewhere by the sea. She had a yellow satin dress well, nylon really, and white frayed knickers. A piece of cord at the back of her neck made her voice happen. Twiddling her arms made her take a few steps, or was meant to, wasn't that easy. Short hair but ever so soft, goldy. At the time she'd seemed real big. I played with her day after day, broke the working parts pretty soon but that didn't matter to me, only to Mum. She went on about how much it'd cost and had warned, 'Wait till your father gets home . . . ' Usually when she said that he ended up doing nothing at all. Didn't appreciate her influence, liked to sort things out his own way. In other words he was dead awkward. Gran says they thrived on their arguments – Gran says too much. This occasion, he did take notice of Mum, solely because of the price. Took the doll away as a punishment for not looking after it properly. Took it right away. Said if I couldn't take care of things then I'd not have them. Never saw it again. Tried everything – being good, throwing a tantrum, nothing changed it. She was gone. And that's how it feels now. Something that belonged to me, no one else, has been snatched away, and I won't pretend it's all right because it isn't.

And don't talk to me about 'time'. Time doesn't heal or fade anything, it teases. If I was bitter at Christmas, then that feeling must have grown a hundred ways stronger. I can't stop it, make it better. I wake up in the night, in the darkness, there's bristles against my skin, spit on my face, pee on my body. Inside my head, he's laughing at me, calls me tramp, dog. I smell him on the sheets where he's been so close, I'm wet and sticky from him, hot, hotter. And I'm so frightened. Of not being tough enough, brave enough, of falling down hard. I'm not ready, but there's no option and I have to be ready. I'm too old, I'm too young.

But I'm going to teach myself to change things.

Mum says that it takes years of practice to grow up. She's pulled herself together, I think for Mikey's sake. I wish that it'd been for herself, just a little bit. She doesn't like her life but she doesn't hate it as much as she used to. Mum's a brave coward. She is herself though. I can't seem to be me. Mum says that if people don't treat you as an equal, then you've got to drag them down to your level. She can do that, but those types can see the guilt in me, I know they can.

We'll manage. We've got a home. More than some people have got. A sort of family. I want something else but don't know if I'll ever get it. I'll take what I consider to be mine. And what's not mine if I want it bad enough. Mum says that you don't find happiness until you stop searching for perfection. I think it's like a war. You think you're safe, then all of a sudden, the guns go bang bang.

Eileen Fairweather

French Letters: The Life and Loves of Miss Maxine Harrison, Form 4a

Teenager Maxine has got REAL problems. She longs for glamour and romance but she's broke, forever on a diet and her best friend has gone to live in Lancashire.

In her almost daily letters to Jean, Maxine moans about the unfairness of parents, and the meanness of older sisters. But the race to get A Real Boyfriend tests their friendship – Jean says that Bunsen Burner Pete is a front runner but Maxine lands a dishy French penfriend with gorgeous eyes (that's *extrêmement romantique* – don't you think?).

THEN she sends him a photo of her slimmer, prettier friend, pretending that it is her, and tells him that her bus conductor dad is Head of London Transport.

THEN a letter arrives from Paris to say he's coming to visit...

PANIC ! ! ! ! ! !

ISBN: 0 7043 4903 5
Fiction £2.95

Kristin Hunter

THE SOUL BROTHERS AND SISTER LOU

For Louretta and her friends, life in a black neighbourhood of a large American city is hard, often violent. Where can they go after school? There's no space at home and the police make it difficult on the streets.

Lou is determined to find a place they can make their own, a clubhouse. But even her natural enthusiasm and sense of fun is almost destroyed when one of their gang is killed right in front of them.

Making music makes life easier though, and as they learn more about the true history of soul, Lou and her friends – even the cynical Fess – find hope for the future.

Long awaited reissue of this sixties American cult novel.

ISBN: 0 7043 4900 0
Fiction £3.50

Angela Martin

YOU WORRY ME TRACEY, YOU REALLY DO

A riotous collection of razor sharp cartoons on:

Famous Problems	Fat thighs, parents, how far to go
Handy Hints	Spots, Hairy legs, little brothers, fashion
Classic Dilemmas	How much can you *really* tell your best friend...
Great Excuses	Staying out late, not doing homework
Top Tips	How to be 'cool'
Famous Crushes	Who you fancy, and who you're *supposed* to fancy...

ISBN: 0 7043 4902 7
Cartoons £1.95

Maude Casey
Over the Water

Mary and her family are going on their annual visit to their family in Kilkenny, Ireland. For her parents it's always exciting, they are 'going home', but Mary doesn't really feel as though she belongs anywhere . . . she feels just as much a stranger in the Irish family home as she does in school in England where her classmates taunt her with anti-Irish jokes and scrutinise her for signs of 'thickness'.

But this summer is a surprise. Mary meets an exciting young aunt now living in New York and finds that through talking with her, and in the stories told by her elderly grandmother and the urgent demands of the family farm, she discovers a new sense of herself, her real history . . . and catches a glimpse of her destiny.

An exciting first novel about being Irish, and Irish in another land.

ISBN 0 7043 4905 1
Teenage fiction £2.95